I'M A MAN

I'M A MAN

STORIES BY

PETER JOHNSON

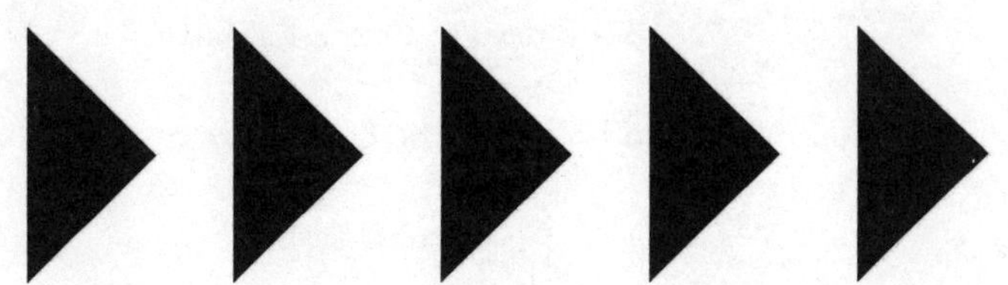

WHITE PINE PRESS • BUFFALO, NEW YORK

WHITE PINE PRESS
P.O. Box 236, Buffalo, New York 14201

Acknowledgments:
"I'm a Man," *Beloit Fiction Journal*; "Ex-Ray," *The Mississippi Review* (finalist for 2001 contest); "Flamenco" and "Shadowboxing," *Treasure House*; "The Angry Man" and "Two Treesomes," *Web del Sol* (webdelsol.com); "Nude Photographs, Obscene Phone Calls," *Five Fingers Review*; "WHOOSH!," *Victory Park*; "The More Things Change," *Controlled Burn*; "Rich Girl" and "A Tradition," *Ducky*; "The Chair," *Alembic.*

"Flamenco,""The Angry Man," "Shadowboxing," "Nude Photographs, Obscene Phone Calls," and "I'm a Man" also appeared in *I'm a Man*, winner of Raincrow Press' 1997 Fiction Chapbook Contest.

Publication of this book was made possible, in part, by grants from the National Endowment for the Arts and with public funds from the New York State Council on the Arts, a State Agency.

Book design: Elaine LaMattina

Printed and bound in the United States of America

First Edition

1 3 5 7 9 10 8 6 4 2

Library of Congress Control Number: 2003108957

Contents ▸ ▸ ▸ ▸ ▸

"They say, best men are moulded out of faults,
And, for the most, become much more better
For being a little bad."

—Mariana to Isabella
Measure for Measure
William Shakespeare

For my family,
especially the boys...

FLAMENCO

▶ ▶ ▶ ▶ ▶

"LEAVE HER ALONE," Dad said. "She's learning something this time."

"She learns something every time," I said, wanting to get under his skin.

"Just remember, Frank, this is my house."

"And a man's home is his castle," I sang, almost adding that while the King was downing a few beers and wondering whether Roger Clemens could hold a two-run lead, El Cobra was in the back room of a West Side bar having his way with Patti. But I tried to be reasonable. "If she could sing, this might make sense, Dad."

"But she must have some talent."

"Have you ever heard her even hum along to the radio?"

"Just give me a cigarette," he said, shaking his head.

I looked at him, seeing more of myself in his eyes than I wanted to. People always said we looked alike; they couldn't even distinguish our voices on the phone. I wanted to move, but someone had to hold things together.

"Go save her if you want to," he said. "But that bar can't let her in, anyway. She's only seventeen."

I gave him a cigarette. "Don't be so sure."

"I just want her to be happy," he said sadly.

"We're already doing a good job. Maybe we should start

introducing her to guys. We know her type, divorced at least six times with weird occupations like dirt-bike racer or middle-aged rock climber. Maybe we should buy some fedoras and drive around in a shiny, pink Cadillac."

"What?"

"Pimps, Dad."

He stood and threw the unlit cigarette onto the floor. "You talk like a pig about your sister," he said. "What's your problem?" He stuck a gnarled index finger into my chest, pushing me backward. "You want me to go hammer what's his face?"

"El Cobra."

"Or break his goddamn fingers, so he can't play the guitar."

"It's a penis, Dad. The guitar's a metaphor."

He took a run at me, grabbing my shirt and shoving me against the wall. "You're sick. You've always thought and talked like we got the wrong kid at the hospital, like you're the kid of some junkie because that's how you think—junk, crap, and more junk. You just make it sound better because you've got college. Did you meet this El Cobra, you big jerk? He was polite. He was a gentleman."

Every time he finished a sentence, he tightened his grip on my shirt, jerking my head back against the wall. He was a boxer in the Navy and could no doubt take care of himself, yet I wasn't afraid. I stood there, daring him to hit me, but he loosened his grip and collapsed onto the recliner.

"You're evil, Frank."

I adjusted my shirt. "Let me tell you something about El Cobra, alias The Dick."

He shook his head. "Do you know what I see, what I imagine?"

"I've been doing some checking," I said. "He's a Wop

but tells everyone he's Spanish and owns a villa in Europe. He's been divorced twice, has three kids from those marriages, and he's currently shacked up with some poor wench who used to sing in his group. He knocked her up."

"Christ," my father said, resting his elbows on his knees, cradling his face in both hands.

"The guy's thirty-six, Dad."

"Jesus," he said, looking up at me. "He seemed like a nice guy. We've got to get her out of there, Frank."

On the drive to Toucan's, the club where Patti was singing, he thanked me for being honest about El Cobra, and I felt bad about that, though it wasn't as if I had totally lied. I was convinced that the truth about El Cobra was worse than anything I could imagine. Granted, I hadn't met him and didn't know if he'd been married, but I knew my sister's type well enough to realize my guesswork was solid. The important point was that if I wanted to rescue Patti, I needed some parental authority with me. I needed the Specter of Guilt, the ineluctable presence of The Father.

El Cobra was more popular than I thought because his performance was sold out, and the bouncer wouldn't let me in without a ticket. I had a notion to return to the car and tell Dad, who had decided to wait outside, that at this very moment Patti was baring her breasts on stage to assorted drunks, which would have agitated him into breaking down the door. But I didn't want to push my luck. I had gotten him to come; if he wanted to wait in the car, that was his business.

But I still had to deal with the bouncer, who had the biceps of Sylvester Stallone and the face of an iguana. I could have told him that he had a seventeen-year-old girl performing in the bar that night, but, instead, I calmly explained that I was the brother of one of the great flamenco singers of all time, who was currently performing with El Cobra and who had promised to leave me a ticket at the door. He looked at me as if I were some bug he was considering for dinner, then let me in, grumbling, "If you screw up, Jack, you're out on your ass."

On my way past him, I said, "If a stocky old guy looking like the Avenging Angel of Death storms the front door, tell him I'll be standing by that big speaker on the left." The bouncer looked at me, trying to decide whether I was ridiculing him. A muscle twitched in his left cheek; he opened his mouth, displaying a blackened set of teeth only a horse doctor could appreciate.

"I'm watching you," he said. "I'm watching you."

I smiled, thinking I could take him if push came to shove. For one thing, I'm big and strong. I'm sure I would have been some big, strong, dumb jerk laying bricks the rest of my life if I didn't have all these strange ideas whanging around inside my head. I'm also invincible when I'm righteous, and I was feeling very righteous that night, being on a mission of some importance. I didn't want to save Patti from herself, which was quite impossible, but I was going to make clear to El Cobra and to any other fast dick in town that to fuck over my sister was to fuck over me. If could make that point with my wits, all the better; if not, I was more than willing to fight someone.

I went to the bar and bought a Rolling Rock, then walked over to a large speaker, searching for a table. Unfortunately, the ones in front were reserved for flamenco aficionados, phonies who had decided it would be cool to be someone else for a night. I recognized a car mechanic I'd gotten stoned with a couple of years before, an Australian, dressed in a white suit, his head topped with a white fedora. He was puffing on a huge Cuban cigar, but his impersonation of Juan Valdez was betrayed by his reddish tan and long, blond locks. He was the kind of jerk Patti liked. When he waved to me, I nodded my bottle his way. I decided to keep an eye on him, but he momentarily disappeared into the swirling smoke. In the four corners of the room, the management had set up miniature search lights that slowly scanned the audience, occasionally crisscrossing each other, cutting swaths of white light through the smoke.

The rumble of small talk quieted down, and, to my left, I saw El Cobra's entourage walking against the wall toward the stage. They were led by El Cobra himself, waving his guitar over his head, acknowledging the applause. Some patrons yelled out Spanish phrases they stole from old Carmen Miranda movies, and I joined in with a few yips and yaps of my own. Patti was the last of the performers, and it was going to be a vintage Patti night. She wore a lightweight, white cotton dress, so when the search lights discovered her, you could see the outlines of her bra and panties. Her long, blond curly hair danced on her shoulders as she hopped behind the other performers. I knew she would attract attention from the male clientele. I knew that when these phony Chiquita bananas saw her, they'd let out a collective loin sigh only her beauty could elicit.

She sat next to two other dark-skinned women on stage, and I had to admire El Cobra's taste. At their feet were instruments—pieces of metal and wood—that I had never seen before, and when the Snake Man started to play, the three women shook and banged the instruments, yelping like a bunch of wounded coyotes. El Cobra himself stood at the microphone fingering and smacking his guitar. He was shorter than I had expected and had hair the color and texture of Patti's. When he started chanting again, the women appeared drugged, glassy-eyed.

After a few songs, El Cobra asked Patti to join him, introducing her as a new member of the group, kissing her paternally on the cheek. The car mechanic stood up, waving his fedora over his head, then bowing at the waist, as if in solemn respect. El Cobra smiled, but I wasn't fooled by these pleasantries.

He continued to speak about his home in Spain, explaining how the next song, which he had written for Patti, was inspired by the "untamed" women of the region. I laughed loudly, receiving a few stares from people around me. El Cobra tried to focus his eyes on the laugh, but the lights blinded him. Patti, too, looked concerned, probably locking onto the familiarity of my laugh, which she loathed more than a Friday night without a date.

There was a moment of silence, then Patti approached the microphone for her solo, while El Cobra began to pick feverishly at his guitar. She stood there, hovering, as if ready for flight, waiting for a sign to begin. She started to sing, to gyrate before El Cobra. I didn't know Spanish or flamenco music, but it wasn't necessary. What she howled was directed only at El Cobra, and the language he had given her sprung from water and dirt—from the muddy old rites of Dionysus. The audience seemed agitated by this musical intercourse, and I thought the whole room was about to erupt into fornication. Mostly, though, I was appalled that my little sister was somehow the source of this spiraling sexuality. I was trying to decide how to handle the situation when I was saved by the Australian, who was beside himself, standing, clapping his hands. And the sight of this ersatz flamenco neophyte enraptured by the orgiastic groans of my seventeen-year-old sister made me laugh. Try as I might, I couldn't stop.

At first Patti attempted to go on, El Cobra so intent on his instrument that no distraction could break his concentration. Then she lost her fervor, and the song came abruptly to an end. El Cobra joined her at the microphone, holding his guitar at his side like a staff. I could feel the growing silence on stage and in the audience, but as long as the mechanic was in sight, I couldn't stop laughing. I heard the audience's outraged comments, including a number of "What's your problem?" and one guy shouting over and over, "Get the asshole outta here. Get the asshole outta here."

When El Cobra asked the stage manager to shine a light on the blasphemer of flamenco, I was momentarily blinded, he and my sister becoming distant silhouettes. Then I heard him—not El Cobra the famous flamenco guitarist, not El Cobra the Latin lover—but El Cobra the working-class Dago from Kenmore, N.Y. "What's the matter with you, Buddy?" he yelled.

"Snake Man," I yelled back, "can you repeat that in the native Spanish of your homeland?"

I was a bit surprised by what happened next. El Cobra, this pygmy-sized gaucho, dropped his guitar and charged me from the stage, with Patti close behind. The stage manager, noticing the action, shifted a different set of lights onto the streaking guitarist and his enraged concubine. When El Cobra got a few feet from me, I reacted instinctively, raising my leg and kicking him in the face.

He went down hard and I was a little worried, thinking flamenco guitarists probably didn't have the strongest neck muscles in the world.

He lay motionless on the floor, but instead of coming

to his aid, Patti barreled into me. She wrapped her arms around my waist, trying to push me backward. I raised my half-finished bottle over my head, holding her tightly to my chest with my other arm. She fought herself free and swiped a beer bottle off a table. I was a bit surprised when she hit me with it, but I knew I wasn't badly hurt, just a warm scar of blood snaking its way down my cheek. Instead of getting mad, I smiled, and I think she would have stabbed me with the broken end of the bottle if the bouncer hadn't intervened. He passed her to another bouncer, then rushed me. He obviously had been looking forward to this confrontation, but much to his disgust, I went limp. It wasn't that I was afraid of him, but I had accomplished my mission and didn't see any reason to fight.

A few minutes later, I was on my ass on the sidewalk outside Toucan's, my beer still in hand, blood trickling down my cheek, old Iguana-face smiling down at me as if he'd just finished his third Big Mac. "You're an asshole, Jack," he said, acting very much the victor, which he would have been, if not for the crazed King of Reckio's Bowling Alley, alias Dad, who was at that moment charging him like a psychotic elephant.

It was no contest.

Dad and the bouncer went hurtling into the smoke-filled twilight of the bar. I saw the event from Dad's point of view: he's stewing in the car for over a half an hour when he looks up and sees his son dragged out of a bar with a head wound.

Knowing Dad could take care of himself, I walked back to the car. Sure enough, about five minutes later, he came out of Toucan's dragging Patti behind him. He threw her into the back seat and we drove off. She cried all the way home, explaining what had happened. As she talked, I felt

Dad looking sideways at me. I knew he would eventually discover that many of the facts I had related about El Cobra weren't exactly true, but I felt confident he would see the soundness of the rescue.

When we got home, he sat with Patti, half-chastising her, half-comforting her. I went into the bathroom and closed the door behind me, working on my face with a washcloth and some peroxide. The door opened and Patti appeared. She stood before me, thigh to thigh, glaring at me, grabbing the washcloth and rubbing it deeply into my open cut. Although it stung mightily, I never blinked, never took my eyes off hers. When she threw the washcloth into the sink, she started to pound on my chest, so I grabbed her arms, pulling her toward me, stroking her hair, and when I looked up, Dad was in the doorway, a look of horror on his face.

"You're a bastard," he said.

I panicked for a moment, then slowly closed the bathroom door with one foot. In time, I knew he'd understand, knew he'd see that someone had to defend what little dignity we had left.

After the fiasco at Toucan's we didn't see Patti for about a week. One night I couldn't relax. It was just me and the Old Man watching a game on TV, making small talk. I left the house and drove to the lakefront, thinking I might take a walk and grab a hot dog from a local vendor.

After I ate, I climbed a tower overlooking Lake Erie. Off to my right, I could see the Niagara River beginning to form; to my left the lights of Pilot Field glowed. I tried hard to think back to happier times, knowing that there were no happier times.

About ten years ago, one damp morning in April, the cops discovered a middle-aged woman face down in the Niagara. As she floated close to shore, a tree branch had reached out and hooked her by the rosary she wore around her neck. The woman was my mother; the rosary was from some shrine in Yugoslavia. The last person to see her, a clerk at Billy's Food Mart, said she had stumbled in drunk from the pouring rain and had given him a holy card of St. Jude. "Praise be to Jesus," she said on her way out. The police found no evidence of foul play; to them, she was just another drunk, another nut case. When my father went to identify her, in one of the dumbest moves of this century, he brought Patti with him. She was only about seven at the time, yet no one stopped her from following him into the room. "Unbelievable" is what I said to the nurse on duty. "Totally unbelievable."

THE ANGRY MAN

▶ ▶ ▶ ▶ ▶

SIX O'CLOCK AND CALEB pulls up, out of breath from his eight-block trip. He does a wheelie, lays a thin, black skid mark on the sidewalk in front of my steps. He's puffing, decked out in army fatigues, green paint slashing his cheeks. "I've got witnesses," he yells. "This old guy grabbed me by the throat. Tommy was there and Enzio. Dad's waiting for you, Uncle Henry. He's going to kick some ass. I've got witnesses." Then he's up on his bike, maneuvering his fat, camouflaged shape down the street, dodging imaginary assailants. It seems the McEachern Clan has been done wrong again, and I'm about to be pressed into duty.

When I arrive at John's house, he and Claudia are going at it on the front porch, real contrasts in shape. John is tall and sorely overweight, but proof you can still live into your mid-forties if you drink, smoke dope, pound nails all day, and cultivate the personal life of a mercenary soldier. Yet Claudia, all five feet of her, has him against the railing, yelling, "Fix the toilet, fix the stove." She walks over to the screen door, and with all the strength she can muster, kicks her foot through it, "Fix the goddamn door, why don't you." She looks sexy, all pumped up, her nipples hard under her Led Zeppelin T-shirt, the white quarter moons of her can quivering below the fringe of her denim shorts. "Henry," she yells at me, "I gotta live in this neighborhood. Make him do something useful with his time."

John locks those disturbed McEachern eyes on me, points a crooked finger in my direction. "Stay out of it," he barks. Then he confronts Claudia, jamming the same finger into her nose, "And you, Little Miss Whore of the World, get inside." I, myself, would've run like hell, but Claudia insists on the last word.

"Bust you," she yells on her way inside, a phrase I never heard before but one obviously holding a special meaning for them.

"Bust you, too," John yells back. "Nobody grabs my kid by the throat."

John looks as if he's just come home from roofing. His hands, arms, and T-shirt are dirty and spotted with tar; his jeans probably haven't been washed in a week. Claudia isn't your basic washing-and-ironing housewife, which led John one day to say he'd be better off with an inflatable doll, though I can't imagine a doll with the sexual gamesmanship Claudia must possess. Looking at John, I'm sad to see he's let himself go. He's still strong but has a beer gut and one of those scraggly beards you see on pig farmers, the kind of lumpy guys who prowl the country roads at night, hoping some pretty girl breaks down.

He's staring at me, disgusted about something. He waves his arms, looking for support from the neighbors, who are probably inside hoping he'll quiet down or drive away. "Check this out, everyone. My brother comes to a fight dressed like a goddamn undertaker. What're you going to do," he says, spreading his arms as if to perform magic, "strangle someone with your tie? I wish Pop could see this."

I want to tell him that I don't roof houses for a living,

that I just got home from teaching summer school, that I was enjoying a cold beer when Rambo Jr. appeared at my door. Instead, I take off my tie and ask what happened.

"You don't have to fight," he says, "just support me, for Christ's sake." At first he wants to take his motorcycle, and I can picture him beginning his attack by laying a twenty-foot skid mark on some poor guy's front lawn, but he decides instead on the red pickup. "Nobody grabs my kid by the throat," he yells. "Nobody."

We speed past houses to the end of the block, make a quick right, and pull up on the front lawn of a brown two-family. John's half out of the truck before it stops, skipping up two stairs at a time to reach an old man sitting on the porch. I'd seen John punch out bikers and humiliate a construction worker by calling him a "faggot" in front of his kids. One night at a bar I saw him drag a drunk who insulted Claudia over to a large whirling fan; he held the guy's face a few inches from the blades until he cried. And, most recently, when an impeccably groomed Yuppie kept beeping at me because I wasn't accelerating quickly enough at a traffic light, John got out of my car and dragged the offender through the open window of his black BMW. He didn't hit him. He just shook him, the way you'd rattle a Coke machine that robbed you of a quarter for the fiftieth time. Then he dropped him onto the road, laughing at the circular stain dampening the crotch of the guy's summer suit. John could do that to you, make you aware of the unpredictability of your bladder and sphincter muscles.

But these guys were around John's age, most of them tough guys themselves, looking for someone to antagonize. In contrast, the man on the porch has to be at least sixty. He's sitting calmly in a rocker, drinking from a can of Budweiser. He's smiling. No neighbors are out, except for a man watering his bushes across the street, and another man, maybe thirty-five, who's walking behind a little boy on a tricycle. But Caleb's there with two other boys, all in camouflage and war paint. One holds a plastic machine gun at his hip, readying himself to shoot down a few pigeons; the other is a nervous little creature fingering his imitation bowie knife.

I jump out of the truck and want to stop John because it doesn't seem right. But he's going after this guy, and it's killing him because he knows he can't hit an old man, or gouge out his eyes. So he starts working him over with his mouth. He begins with, "No one grabs my kid by the throat," and goes on from there. He's going to do something to the guy's balls, his knees, his kids' balls, and by God, he'll burn this guy's house down. John's face is about two inches from the old man's, but the old man doesn't flinch, and you'd think John was asking him for directions to Wilson Farms.

This surprises John and he keeps talking, prefacing everything he says with "Fucking-A" this and "Fucking-A" that, which makes the man walking his little boy pause. And this worries me. I move toward him wanting to explain that John says "Fucking-A" with the regularity most people say, "You know." If John were into Transcendental Meditation, no doubt the Swamis would have given him "Fucking-A" as his mantra. But this guy's thinking, I know what he's thinking: don't talk like that in front of my kid; don't violate my neighborhood with that language. And I know if some guy were spouting this garbage on John's street, John would be the first one to take a utility knife to his tongue.

But how do I explain John to him? I see this man can take care of himself if pushed too far, tap some reserve, like those women who pick up the front ends of cars their kids are trapped under. He's checking out John and me; he's wearing jeans and a blue T-shirt. His chest makes slight heaves, his body priming itself for trouble, his heart filling, a thousand pinpricks awakening his scalp. Every guy who has been brave or scared shitless has experienced this rush. John seeks it on a daily basis.

But this man is also hesitating, as if he wants to talk sense to John, appeal to some innate goodness we're supposed to have. He doesn't realize that, to John, he's nothing more than some "Fucking-A" something or other blocking a pattern of revenge as old as the McEachern Clan.

I want to tell him, "If you want a piece of him, sneak up while he's yelling at the old man, and hit him from behind. Then if he tries to get up, keep smashing him." But he wouldn't listen. There's a look of intelligence in his face, which will be his downfall if John's anger turns his way. Guys have been fighting since Day One, yet so few of them know what to do. In the movies, you see James Bond come back from the dead time after time by doing things like sucking the air out of tires while hiding underwater. If John were the villain in a Bond movie, he'd handle things differently. He'd put a few exploding bullets in his Magnum, walk over to James, and blow his head off.

For a moment everything seems to freeze, except for John pacing back and forth across the porch, savagely stroking his beard, seeming to realize that he might as well be screaming at a cigar store Indian. He looks at Caleb. "This better be the real deal," he says, and Caleb gestures to his fellow guerrillas for support. Then John lets out this unnatural groan, leaning over and spitting on the old guy's shoes.

"I spit on you," he says. "I spit on your family." Then

he repeats everything he said earlier, raising his voice with each "Fucking-A."

"Now see here," the man with the little boy says.

Caleb's all over him. "Stay out of it. Fend to your own business."

I'm wondering if I should be saying this. Where did Caleb, who has trouble with the concept of a homonym, come up with "Fend to your own business"?

Two fortunate things happen to the man. First, his child begins to cry, which distracts him; secondly, the front door of the house next door opens and a young woman appears. She's tiny, looks Italian or Portuguese, and seems very tired. But she's young, and undoubtedly would be a dazzler with a nap and a little eye shadow. She's holding a large fork with a hot dog impaled on it, as if in the middle of barbecuing she heard one too many "Fucking-A's."

Behind her, protected by the screen door, is a large man. Her husband? Her boyfriend? I don't know. He doesn't come out of the house, but I hear him trying to persuade her back to the grill. She ignores him, watching John, who seems oblivious to her.

She's waving the fork over her head. "Hey," she yells. "Hey, Mr. Crazy Man."

John stops and looks at her.

"Leave," she yells.

"What?"

"Leave. The boys ran through his backyard and messed up his garden, so he grabs the fat one by the shirt. Big deal. Go home. Take a pill."

A big hairy arm appears from behind the door and tries to pull the woman in, but she shakes it off. "Enough," she says wearily. "Enough."

Caleb's shaking his fist in the air. "Stay out of it. Fend

to your..."

"Shut up, Caleb," John says, and walks down the steps, moving toward the lady with a look of perplexity.

The man leaves his crying child, placing himself between John and the woman, and the man with the hairy arm comes from behind the screen door and stands next to her. Neither one of them realizes that John could cripple them within seconds, so I intervene.

"John?"

"What do you want?" he growls, as if I had just shown up by accident.

"Let's leave."

He looks at me, appears offended, shocked. "You think I'd smack a woman," he says, then pushes me to the ground. When I look up, I'm at the feet of one of Caleb's accomplices, who's trying to figure out if there's a way he can maim me and stay out of my class next year.

I'm up quickly, though, not trusting John, doing something I didn't think myself capable of. I throw myself at him, trying to push him down, and with him, Pop and the memory of every battle I've ever been witness to. I strain, smelling sweat and tar, but can't lock my hands around his massive gut. I wait for men to rush from their houses and jump on this bully. But nothing happens. John laughs, then shoves me to the ground again, and I look up to see the back of his dirty hand just before it stings my cheek.

Something goes out of John after he hits me. "You gotta understand, lady," he says.

She points to the truck. "Go, angry man. Enough."

John looks at her, then at the man next to her, and to everyone's surprise, he walks back to his truck and hops in. The man just nods, probably thinking he'll treat his woman right for the rest of the week, considering she saved his ass from John.

When John leans over to close the passenger door, our eyes meet. I hope blood is streaming down my chin. I want him to feel guilty. But he just shakes his head and smiles, then closes the door, backing off the grass and driving slowly away. Within moments, the guerrillas are on their bikes, following the blood-red truck like a pack of mosquitoes.

I stand and look at the old man, then all around me. Everyone's waiting for me to say something. "You should've gone into the house," I explain. "When a guy explodes like that, you have to walk away."

The old man smiles, takes a hit from his beer, and spits over the railing into the bushes. "I think he had the wrong guy," he says.

I look at the woman for support. "Both of you should be ashamed of yourselves," she says.

Then doors open, and men appear on porches talking to each other. "He's my brother," I say, not knowing whether I'm offering a defense or an apology. But no one responds, so I jog back to John's house and drive home.

Tonight is beautiful, a cool, dry, late August evening given sound to by the bony legs of crickets. It's nine-thirty when I go into my study and open the family photo album for about the thirtieth time this year, scanning pictures of me and John, me and Pop, John and Pop, and all three of us. In one picture, we're leaning against a wire-mesh backstop. Pop is between me and John, his hairy arms drawing us into him. He and John are smiling at each other, while I'm standing up, arms limply at my side, head down, as if I'd just peed my pants and Pop and John are having a good laugh over it. In the picture, I'm eight, John is ten. I'm wearing my baseball uniform, Rocky's

Cleaners etched in white print across my chest. We had just lost the championship of the 8-10-year-old division. In the last inning, we were down by one run and the bases were loaded. I was up at the plate and Pop was coaching third. He called time out and we met halfway down the third base line. "Swing at the first three pitches," he said. "One of them will be a beauty." For the whole game, he'd been watching the opponent's pitcher and realized that two out of the first three pitches were always strikes. I went back to the plate and looked dumbly at the first three pitches. All were strikes and the game was over. Afterwards, I wanted to tell Pop that I tried to move my arms but couldn't, that I was scared and didn't know if it was worse to take three strikes or swing three times and miss, which I would have done. Although he never questioned me, when I look at the picture now, his and John's smiles seem conspiratorial.

It's eleven p.m. I'm a little drunk when I get into my car and drive to John's neighborhood. I park two blocks from his house and walk the rest of the way, the hazy lights of televisions guiding me. When I get to his place, I crouch behind the back of his pickup and duckwalk forward. All the lights are off except for one in the bedroom. I know it's the bedroom light because it's red; I know that sexual shenanigans are taking place because I can hear Led Zeppelin's first album. I shared an apartment with John when we were younger so I know his rituals, know he'll have a glass of whiskey poured, know he'll make Claudia put on makeup before he'll make love to her.

I crawl to the back of the truck and feel around coils of ropes and blunt ends of tools until I lay my hands on something weighty, a large wrench. When I return to the front, I feel ashamed, cowardly. Screw you, I think, standing up and bringing the wrench down into the right front headlight.

From behind, I hear, "Fucking-A," and I know I should run, but instead go after the other light, taking it out with two blows, dropping the wrench, promising myself not to turn around. Be brave, you bastard, I think. Be a man. I walk slowly to the end of the driveway, imagining John crashing through the front door, gripping his Magnum, or maybe his hunting knife. Then I jog to the end of the block and make a left turn, picking up speed, pushing off from a light pole with my right foot, and I'm off down another street, running as fast as I can.

NUDE PHOTOGRAPHS, OBSCENE PHONE CALLS

BOBBY'S STORY, THE ONE about Stan, went like this:

Thursday morning, Bobby was working on the shears when the break horn sounded. He continued to finish an order. That's just the way he was. As he slid the last few bars over the rollers, measuring them for a cut, he looked up and saw some guys surrounding Stan's locker located near the plant's entrance. They were passing around color photographs. Some guys were whistling, others laughing or slapping their thighs. Most of them still wore their work hats and goggles, but Stan had removed his, so Bobby could see his red, curly hair bobbing and weaving among the men as he pointed to this photograph or that, giving a thumbs up or thumbs down signal. He flashed a crazy grin, working the men like a preacher.

Bobby finished his measurements and was about to make his last cut when he heard yelling. It appeared that there was a fight between Stan and a crane operator named Louis Burnham, but no punches were being thrown. Burnham had Stan pinned against a locker, holding him by both shirt pockets, and although Burnham was a short, overweight guy and Stan was tall and muscular (a good street fighter as a kid), Burnham seemed in control. He slammed Stan against the locker once, twice. On the third slam, he lost his balance, falling forward on Stan, chest to chest, their combined weight bringing down an entire row of metal lockers. For a moment, all Bobby saw were guys circling the action, frozen by the unexpected fight. A cloud of dirt and ore dust rose from the center of the circle, the harsh steel plant lights making the metallic flakes glow like fireflies.

Bobby shut down his machine and ran toward the cloud, but by the time he got there two guys had pulled Burnham off Stan and were restraining him. Burnham was still wild with anger, his face made weird and frightening by the steamy goggles he wore. He tried to shake off the men, but they held him by each arm, while Stan still lay on the lockers, appearing more dumbfounded than hurt, the dust from the crash all over his face. He held some photographs in one hand, while the others were scattered around the toppled lockers.

Bobby expected Stan to get up and smack Burnham, but instead he kept apologizing to him, and then to everyone. "I didn't know," he said. "I didn't know."

The apology seemed to calm Burnham, though when the two men released him, he did something strange and very sad. He walked over to his locker, opposite to where Stan was before the fight, and sitting down on a grey wooden bench, he cried into both hands, chanting over and over, "Jesus, Jesus, Jesus...."

Bobby had never seen a grown man cry in front of so many other men, and the rest of the guys also seemed embarrassed. Finally, Burnham stood, and without speaking to anyone, walked out of the plant.

After he left, Bobby picked up a photograph and realized what had happened. Stan had often told Bobby about the women he slept with, and Bobby didn't mind, since it made him remember his own bachelor days. One day, over at Stan's apartment, Stan said he had pictures of girls he'd been with—not all of them, just the ones he had photographed nude. He said it turned them on and was cheaper than Quaaludes. After he took a girl's picture, he and the girl would look at it (he had one of those cameras that developed pictures on the spot), and then they'd make love. He asked Bobby if he wanted to see the pictures—he might even know some of the girls—but Bobby felt funny about the whole business. Stan called him a prude, but that wasn't it at all. As a matter of fact, Bobby appreciated the genius of the idea, and since his conversation with Stan, he often imagined taking pictures of certain women or teenaged girls on his block. He had even invented elaborate poses for each one.

Unfortunately for Stan, on Thursday morning when he showed these pictures to the other guys, it turned out one of the girls was Burnham's daughter. Stan swore he didn't know. "I picked her up at a bar," he explained, still sprawled on his back. "We didn't talk much. I didn't even know her last name. What lousy luck."

The other guys didn't seem angry at Stan, though they didn't help him up either. They also lost interest in the photographs, perhaps afraid they'd spot a familiar face.

On the Friday night after the Burnham fight, Stan came over to Bobby's for dinner. It was a ritual of sorts. Bobby often thought it strange that Stan, the self-proclaimed womanizer, the Sultan of Snatch, as he called himself, enjoyed having dinner with a married couple every Friday night. But it did seem that way, and Mary Ellen liked having him. She said she felt sorry for Stan because he was single, so she worked hard to make a good meal. She'd be singing while she cooked, and she always prepared a special dessert—pecan pie or cream puffs.

Stan, for his part, always bought a bottle of expensive

red wine that the liquor store owner picked out for him. Bobby knew this, though Mary Ellen thought Stan's "good taste" accounted for the wine. He'd show up at the door, his mouthful of teeth working overtime, asking Bobby what the "little woman" made tonight. Lasagna? Leg of lamb? Potato pancakes?

During the course of these Friday nights, Stan would never fail to mention how lucky Bobby was to have found Mary Ellen. "I'd settle down like that," he'd say, snapping his fingers, smiling and winking at her, "if I could find a woman like you." He'd also congratulate Bobby on having a good son in Little Bobby, not to mention a nice spread. "That's what it's all about," he'd say, a look of loss clouding his face.

Thinking about his life, Bobby had to agree. He was lucky. But it still annoyed him when Stan overdid the flattery, like holding Mary Ellen's chair for her when she sat down for dinner, or insisting on serving the dessert while Mary Ellen had her after-dinner cigarette. Bobby saw it like this: Stan came over one night a week, treated Mary Ellen like a queen, then she expected Bobby to act like that all week.

One Friday night after Stan went home, Mary Ellen said she was surprised no one had latched onto Stan. "He's certainly a hunk," she said, "and he's handy around the house." Bobby didn't want to bad-mouth Stan but he reminded her of Stan's flings, pointing to the real reason Stan wasn't married: he liked to fool around. All she could say was, "I think there's a lot more to Stan than you give him credit for."

The Friday night after the Burnham fight wasn't too different from previous ones. Stan arrived with his bottle of expensive wine, and Mary Ellen made lasagna with Italian sausage and for dessert, cream puffs. They ate dinner around six o'clock, and after Little Bobby went to bed, they spent the rest of the night drinking wine and playing Monopoly. Stan landed on Park Place and Boardwalk early, eventually bought Pennsylvania, North Carolina, and Pacific Avenues off Mary Ellen (for what Bobby thought too cheap a price), and won the game shortly after when he built hotels on his block. It was one of those games where Bobby stayed in jail whenever he could.

Stan left around midnight, and Bobby and Mary Ellen sat at the dining-room table, finishing a bottle of their own wine. The Monopoly board was still opened, Stan's red hotels a reminder of his victory. It had been a good night, everyone cracking jokes, hiding five hundred dollar bills in their pockets or down their pants. At one point, Stan even pulled one out of his fly

Bobby looked across the table at Mary Ellen, glad he had married her. Thirty-two and not a wrinkle on her face. When he first met her he thought she looked like one of those Mediterranean girls he had romanced while in the service—green eyes, olive skin, long black hair. But her sexuality went beyond looks. It was more like a scent that still made Bobby catch his breath. Theirs had been a very carnal courtship, and they had left the heat of their sex all over a city far away from this one—on empty benches, in an elevator once, even in a phone booth one rainy summer night.

Thinking of these nights, Bobby had the urge to make love to her right there on the dining-room table, but she seemed preoccupied. She was smiling, "I hope we always have these Friday nights," she said. "I had so much fun tonight."

Bobby thought about Stan coming over every Friday night for the next twenty years and couldn't muster up much enthusiasm for the idea. He liked Stan, but knew he had faults, like what happened at the plant the day before, and as they packed away the Monopoly game and cleaned up, he told Mary Ellen the story. When he got to the part about the photographs, she looked stunned and dropped one of their new wine glasses onto the hardwood floor.

Was it because she was shocked or just plain disgusted? He didn't know, but he was sorry he had brought it up. He thought she understood Stan, but it was obvious that despite her knowledge of his philandering, she had conjured up a choirboy image of him. Having destroyed that image once and for all, Bobby suddenly felt the need to defend his friend. He told Mary Ellen not to think poorly of Stan; he was only giving these girls what they wanted. "What do you expect," he said, feeling very moral. "That kind of girl deserves that kind of treatment."

"Shut up," she yelled, ending the conversation.

Bobby was surprised because Mary Ellen certainly wasn't a prude. When he first met her in a San Diego bar and later went home with her, he guessed by the way she handled herself in bed that she'd been around. But it didn't bother him because he knew he wouldn't have to deal with her past. When he got out of the service he planned to move back to Buffalo where a job in the plant was waiting for him. Sometimes, though, when Stan would go on about what a "princess" Mary Ellen was, he felt like saying, "Okay, I'm lucky. She's a good wife but there's a lot of things you don't know about her."

After Mary Ellen cleaned up the broken wine glass, she wouldn't talk to Bobby for the rest of the night, and in bed when he turned off the lamp, she inched her ass away from him. At that moment, the gap of silence between them seemed like miles. Bobby took a half hour to nod off, cursing Stan and his own big mouth as he wandered from one bad dream to the next. In the morning, Mary Ellen didn't speak to him until they were having breakfast with Little Bobby. Bobby was reading the sports page of the morning paper when she finally came out with it. "I don't want him here anymore," she said.

"Who?" Little Bobby asked.

"None of your business. Just eat," Mary Ellen said.

Bobby closed the paper, watching Little Bobby wolf down his last few spoonfuls of cereal and grab his baseball hat off the kitchen doorknob on the way out. Bobby didn't look at Mary Ellen until he saw the screen door close. She was staring into her coffee cup, and he felt sorry for her. He reached across the table and touched her hand, trying to console her. "Relax, it's Saturday."

"I just don't want him here."

"How do I tell him?"

"That's your problem. He's your friend."

"He's our friend," Bobby said. "Why don't you tell him?"

"Maybe I will," she said, more to herself than to Bobby. "Maybe I will."

Before Bobby could convince her to forget the story she left the kitchen, abandoning a warm, half-filled cup of coffee. Bobby wasn't angry, because he knew it was more than the Burnham story that ached her. Even before last night, she'd been upset about obscene phone calls she'd been receiving. During the day when Bobby was at work, a guy would call. One day Bobby came home for lunch in the middle of such a call. When he walked into the living room, he saw Mary Ellen sitting on the couch with the phone to her ear. Her face was flushed and she looked like she was in a trance. When she saw him, her body seemed to convulse, and she almost fell off the couch. She yelled something into the mouthpiece, hung up the phone, and began to cry.

Bobby comforted her, suggesting that she hang up right away when she recognized the voice, and she agreed that sounded like a good idea. He also wanted to call the cops, but she said she'd feel silly telling them about it. She wouldn't even tell Bobby what the guy said, though from the look on her face, it must've been some pretty sick stuff. One night he lay in bed, wondering whether the guy was black or white? Did he have a job? Was he married? He wondered if he, too, could be an obscene phone caller, thinking of the women he'd call, of the things he'd say. But he ended up finding the whole idea disgusting. And the more he thought about the caller, the harder it was for him to sleep. Wide-eyed, he tossed and turned most of the night away.

Because the calls seemed to bother him as much as they did Mary Ellen, Bobby sympathized with her for overreacting to the Burnham story. She obviously wasn't herself, so he decided to back off, hoping she'd calm down. And by next Friday she had, though Bobby noticed that the chemistry between her and Stan had definitely changed. After dinner, Stan insisted on helping Mary Ellen serve dessert, and while Bobby set up Monopoly in the living room, he could hear her berating Stan in the kitchen. It was strange listening to her yell at another man, and, in a way, Bobby thought it funny that Stan wasn't defending himself. He wanted to place his ear to the thin wooden, swinging door separating the kitchen from the living room, but instead kept his ground, and when Stan and Mary Ellen returned to the living room, he pretended everything was fine, convincing himself that what was between them was their business. He had a gut feeling, anyway, that the friendship they all shared would eventually win out, though Stan still seemed angry when he sat down to play. He glared at Bobby, and both he and Mary Ellen weren't completely themselves for the rest of the night. Bobby happily realized this when he was able to bankrupt them in only two hours.

But although Bobby knew things would calm down between Mary Ellen and Stan, he wasn't so optimistic about the obscene phone calls. Mary Ellen hadn't discussed the problem, but Little Bobby had been home when they came and he confided in his father. Bobby wasn't mad at Mary Ellen. He thought she lied about the calls because she didn't want to upset him. Nevertheless, it was time to take matters into his own hands. Little Bobby had told him that lately the calls came right after he went to work, so he devised a plan. He wanted to answer the phone and scare the guy. He had heard that obscene phone callers were usually wimps, who wouldn't know what to do with a woman if they had one, so he was going to force this jerk to hear a real man's voice.

One morning, halfway to work, he turned back. This was the day. If the man called, he'd be there waiting. When he arrived, Mary Ellen wasn't in the kitchen. He walked into the living room, but she wasn't there either, and it looked like Little Bobby had left for school. But then he heard her voice upstairs. She was yelling at someone. He tried to make out her excited words, but couldn't. He looked at the phone squatting on the edge of the end table and he sat down on the couch, thinking how strange and unfamiliar her voice sounded. Breathing in deeply, he took a handkerchief from his back pocket and covered the mouthpiece of the receiver, resting it on his lap for a moment. Then he brought it to his ear, waiting to hear the man's voice, wondering if the sickness of this stranger's mind would match his own imaginings of it.

But Mary Ellen was doing most of the talking. She

sounded nervous, yet also cocky, as she asked the man if he owned a camera. "You'd probably be too spooked to take a picture, anyway," she laughed.

"I'd manage," the man replied, in a voice that surprised Bobby because of its reserve.

"Shut up," Mary Ellen said. When she paused, the man laughed, and Bobby tried unsuccessfully to place the laugh, then gently lowered the receiver onto his lap. He wanted to hang up, to slam down the receiver, but he couldn't. He thought of Stan's pictures, of the humiliated Louis Burnham crying into his hands, and he wanted to yell at the caller, or run upstairs and slap Mary Ellen as hard as he could. But more than anything he felt the need to hear her talk, to hear everything and imagine it all with her. To imagine this man imagining it with her and, like this man, to be badgered and seduced at the same time. And this was the impulse that won out in him as he again brought the receiver to his ear. He heard Mary Ellen's voice, gruff, taunting, saying things he had never dreamed her capable of.

SHADOWBOXING

I'M TELLING MY STORY to this couple who are over for dinner, they're friends, though not best friends anymore, more likely over to check out my new wife. I used to be close to them but found out they dropped acid one night, then crawled around on the floor with their two year old. That turned me off. People my age, especially women, are very strange, and that's why I married again and again, and why my new wife is so easygoing, and young, she's only eighteen, and, like I said, that's probably why this couple is over.

I describe the morning my story begins, how I go to the DMV, how there's this guy waiting an hour with the rest of us to renew his license, how when his time comes to get his picture taken, he says, in a very effeminate voice, that he'll come back after his cold goes away. After his cold goes away? That's what I think. And that's what the clerk asks. He tells the clerk his face is puffy, that he has a bad cold and won't walk around for five years (that's how long your license lasts in this state) with a picture that doesn't "reflect" (his word) the way he really looks. Frankly, I didn't care if he had a Mohawk and 15,000 zits, I just wanted out of there. I'd had it with the other flunkies in line, mostly foreigners who couldn't speak English, yet in a matter of hours would be driving all over the state. This guy behind me, a tall, fat guy wearing a beat-up Buffalo Bisons hat, must've had it too, because when the man with the cold leaves, he mumbles, "Faggot," which startles me. I turn around, and he says, "You have a problem with that?" "No sir," I say. But I'm lying. I saw no reason for that comment, I'm almost a college graduate, I have some sensitivity. I've also had first-hand dealings with homosexuals, and I tell my company (the couple who're over to look at my young wife) that I don't hate gays, to remember that because it relates to the mess I'm in, to the story I'm about to tell.

That's not to say I haven't had my moments with homosexuals. In my neighborhood, they're all over the place. They bought up all the two- and three-family houses and jammed them with other homosexuals. And there's a garage sale every time you turn around, but who's in a big hurry to buy silverware or a set of wineglasses off these guys. I've already had three HIV tests. But what I don't like is when they mess with my space. I'm tall and attractive, I attract attention from women. When I explain this to my friends, they laugh because they know what I'm like. But I guess I also attract attention from certain men. One night, walking past CVS, I lit up a cigarette and this guy approaches, starts to talk, you know, what a nice night, this is a great neighborhood, things like that. Then he asks for a smoke, and I light one for him, then he asks what I'm doing, and I begin to see the light, get a little mad, think about having his cigarette in my mouth. "I'm out for a walk," I say. "Christ." But his back's up too, maybe he had a fight with his boyfriend, or is mad because the Irish homosexuals weren't allow to march in the St. Patrick's Day Parade, whatever, and he tells me I'm homophobic, probably not aware I know the meaning of that word. Considering my history with a certain homosexual, I'm very angry, so I explain I don't hate homosexuals, I just don't like jerks, and he's certainly a jerk. (This makes my friend's wife laugh, and my new wife laughs too, though she doesn't know where I'm going with this.) I also tell this specific homosexual that I'd be mad if a guy came onto a woman outside CVS. It's inappropriate. Plain and simple. But the story I'm about to tell isn't about CVS, it concerns an accident.

Last Friday my new wife and I had tickets for a play starring Olympia Dukakis, the woman who was in *Moonstruck*. I always make sure I go to the theater once a year, I did with my first wife, my second wife, and now with my third wife, it's something I think a man and a woman should do together, it's culture. You can't go to the theater alone, or with another guy. Are you supposed to call up a friend and say, "Malcolm, (that's my friend's name, so he laughs), would you like to accompany me to the theater?" It doesn't quite work.

So my new wife and I are excited about the play, but then it starts to snow, so we go back and forth, should we leave or stay home and watch TV, back and forth, back and forth, because we know that even people in Buffalo freak out when it snows. But we decide to go, we're all showered, dressed to kill, ready to attract attention, and, except for my brother's shotgun wedding in Fredonia, we haven't been out in a month. Right before we leave, it starts coming down, and I begin to grumble, but I'm committed. There's about an inch of snow on our street so I take two cinder blocks out of the trunk of my new wife's Escort and throw them into the back of my New Yorker for traction. But things improve as we hit a hill on Delaware Avenue, the pavement worn clean by traffic. We cruise, laughing, I lean over and kiss her, she says something nice, then it all happens.

For some reason, the other side of the hill is as slick as a baby's bum, and this jerk in front me, like so many jerks in this state, starts braking and braking and braking, like that's going to stop him, and his car turns sideways just in time for me to glide into it. My new wife starts screaming, and I'm pissed off, knowing that my insurance will go up about eight thousand dollars. But I try to be cool, maybe work out something with him. He's out of his car sooner than I expect, and in a short time, I'm hitting him, at first in the face, then all over, and that's why I'm telling this story to my friends, to explain the trouble I'm in, to tell them I left out something very important, something about my first-hand dealings with homosexuals.

You see, I didn't visit this couple for a while, it was during a period of heavy drinking, when I lived with a woman who ended up being a little crazy, punching out walls, things like that. (This confession quiets my friends, and my new wife holds my hand.) During this period, I discovered this woman had lived with a homosexual, though she said he was bisexual at the time, but who knows what to believe, because she was still friends with him while she was living with me. And I dug this woman, so I accepted the situation, having the guy over for dinner, one night all of us going to the movies, like he was a brother-in-law, or an uncle. I just blocked it out. Then I learned they were more than friends, so I left, but I had to deal with some pretty unpleasant ideas, and here's when I don't go into details because how do I tell people who're over for dinner about the things I imagined. But I do explain that I'm still pretty angry, about the boozing, about the screwing around, about the HIV tests. Then comes the end of my story, the guy I punched out was the same homosexual or bisexual, have it your way, who went out with my old girlfriend. When he got out of his car and I recognized him, I popped him, just once, but then it felt so good, I kept popping him, again, and again.

As I tell this part of the story, I'm on my feet, shadowboxing in my own living room, my new wife looking a little afraid, but my friends acting very sympathetic. You see, I go way back with them, they know how I react to situations, the way I think.

It takes some getting used to.

WHOOSH!

▶ ▶ ▶ ▶ ▶

TO TOBY, IT WAS MORE of a grinding than a whoosh sound, this hurtling through space. On one trip, the plane's cabin had filled with oily black smoke, and the flight attendant had assured everyone it was just a matter of blowing out the dark cloud—the smoke itself to be absorbed by the white billows below. That time, Toby was flying by himself, composing lists of his strengths and weaknesses on a pad of yellow paper. He knew his real self straddled the black line separating the two lists, one foot in the weakness column, the other in the strength column, both heels resting precariously on banana peels. If the plane had gone down that day over Poughkeepsie or Albany, Toby would have been the only passenger smiling.

Today he found himself again off to the left of center, foggy as the world below. In place of his lists, Max sat on his lap, engrossed in a picture book.

To Max, it was a whoosh. The picture book was opened to the section on airplanes, and Max, his lips pursed, blew out gusts of air, pointing to each aircraft. "Cargo plane," he said. "Passenger plane. Jet fighter. Whoosh."

"Good, Max, very good," Toby said. Toby knew he was a good father, even if half the time he was as disoriented as a newborn kitten.

Normally when Toby and Max flew, people made a fuss over Max, but the man next to them hadn't said a word. About twenty years older than Toby, he was a type Toby called "mechanics"—those anonymous men in pinstriped suits, white shirts, and red ties traveling from city to city, selling everything from water pumps to buttons, carrying their briefcases, which they'd open after the plane reached a certain height. Toby had always admired their shirts—white as a priest's cassock, starched, as if they slid into them right before boarding the plane. But their occupations frightened him, and he believed no one could be happy with jobs like theirs. He imagined them having anxiety attacks before each appointment, waking up in the middle of the night in a cold sweat, gobbling antacid pills like Reese's Pieces.

He moved Max from his lap onto the empty seat by the window. He slid the book into the pouch in front of him, then released his and Max's trays, accidentally bumping the man with his elbow. The man stopped writing on a pad and looked up, more amused than annoyed.

"Sorry," Toby said.

"No problem," the man replied, closing his briefcase and sliding it under the seat in front of him. He also dropped his tray.

"Where're you heading?" Toby asked.

"Toronto," the man responded.

"You're a businessman, aren't you?"

The man smiled. "Yes, I am."

"You know, I always thought that'd be a tough life," Toby said. He pointed to Max. "Max and I see a lot of businessmen when we fly, and I think it must be difficult, especially as you get older."

The man squinted at Toby, sizing him up. "I don't mind."

Toby thought he missed the point. "I mean, traveling all the time, not to mention competing against all those gung-ho kids coming out of college."

The man grimaced. "You've got some curious ideas about business."

"I'm not criticizing."

"I understand, but what do you know about the business world?"

Toby thought for a second. "I know it's not for me, the nine-to-five routine, being told by bosses what to do, always afraid I'll say the wrong thing. Did you ever read *Death of a Salesman*?"

The man laughed.

"Am I wrong?"

The man shook his head. "Yeah, but it's not worth going into."

"That's cool."

The man looked behind him, as if impatient for the stewardesses to arrive. Max kept moving his tray up and down, and Toby tried to calm him. He turned to the man again. "You travel a lot?" he asked, for the first time looking closely at the man's face. He had gray hair around the temples, a strong jaw, and a pug nose. Toby thought he was probably a rugged college football star whose reputation some company had been milking for the last thirty years.

"Do you travel a lot?" the man asked back.

"Just to Buffalo, so Max can see his grandparents."

"Ah," he said. "A divorced dad."

"What?"

"I mean, where's your wife?"

"I'm divorced."

"I knew it," he said, nodding as if something suddenly made sense.

"But Max and I are still a family," Toby said. "I actually spend more time with him than most fathers. I just about raised him the last three years."

"What job lets you do that?"

"I paint."

"Like Degas? Monet?"

"No, like Sherwin-Williams." When Toby laughed, Max grabbed him by the arm, asking for his blanket. Toby reached underneath the seat for a diaper bag, pulling out a blue blanket, and Max collapsed onto it.

"Well, it certainly seems like you know what you're doing," the man said.

"Do you have children?" Toby asked.

"Three, two in college right now, though I didn't have the luxury of staying home with them." The man was smiling, but Toby could tell he was annoyed.

"It's not like I chose to do it," he said.

"Everyone make choices, son."

"Not in this case. Max's mother and I were married ten years before we had him."

"Impressive," the man said.

"I always thought of my wife and I in our sixties, sitting on our porch, watching our kids wrestling outside, you know, living the good life."

"But instead here you are wet-nursing a little boy and painting houses."

Toby flinched. "Like I said, I had a dream of the perfect family, and it took me a year of therapy to realize there were different kinds of families."

The man squirmed in his seat. "Did your wife go to therapy, too?"

"She didn't believe in it."

"Bravo for her."

"What?"

"Just forget it."

"No, what do you mean?"

The man turned sideways in his seat, fixing his eyes on Toby. "Listen, you say you have this dream where you're watching your children frolicking in the leaves, yet you're working as a house painter. How were you going to buy that house or send all those kids to college, and why did you wait ten years to have children?"

"We weren't ready."

The man seemed incredulous. "For what? No offense, Jack."

"My name's Toby."

"No offense, Toby, but something's wrong with this picture."

"You don't know the whole story."

The man sat back in his seat. "Okay, Toby, let's hear it."

Toby glanced at the stewardesses, who were still a number of rows back. "I've always been kind of laid-back," Toby explained, "but that never bothered my wife. We liked the same things and always had enough money to live on. But after Max was born, she didn't want to work and she asked me to take this job I would've hated."

"Why?"

"Because I'd have to suit-and-tie it every day. Nothing personal, but I needed more freedom."

"Like the freedom that comes from painting houses?"

"Yeah."

The man laughed.

"What's so funny?"

"Forget it," he said. "Why don't you check Max's diaper."

"Why are you so bent out of shape?"

"You're the guy who wanted to unload your life," the

man said. “I’m just some dumb bunny in a suit and tie trying to put his kids through college.”

“But you like what you do.”

“Sorry, Toby, but I’m with your wife. You were just afraid to suck it up.”

“But it could’ve worked.”

“No way. She wanted to stay home, make brownies, you know, all that terrible stuff.”

“I never said that.”

“I would’ve liked to have been a little fly on the wall.”

“I tried everything,” Toby complained. “Do you know what it’s like when your wife’s out screwing an insurance salesman while you’re home baby-sitting a little kid?”

The man looked surprised. “She had an affair with an insurance executive?”

Toby felt vindicated. “Yeah.”

“You pushed her that far? Jesus, Toby.”

Toby was astonished.

“What could she do? What choices did she have?”

“Man, this is weird.”

“I agree. It’s a sad story.”

“You don’t know anything,” Toby said.

“I believe you’re a good father, Toby. You’re probably at least that.”

“You don’t know squat, man,” Toby said, feeling himself shaking.

“That’s cool,” the man said, seeming to mimic Toby. Then they both sat quietly for some of the longest minutes Toby could remember.

When the stewardesses arrived, Toby and the man passed on breakfast, and Toby returned his and Max’s trays to the upright position. Max began to stir, and Toby rubbed his back, but instead of going to sleep, Max crawled onto Toby’s lap. “I love you, Daddy,” he said.

Toby felt vindicated, knowing that the man saw and heard everything.

But then the man surprised Toby by leaning over and tickling Max under the chin. "What's up, Max?" he said. Max laughed and attempted to explain his airplane book, while Toby tried to restrain him.

"He really needs a nap," Toby said. But Max grabbed the book and handed it to the man, who opened it, saying that he used to fly planes in the Navy. Resting his head on the man's shoulder, Max gazed at him as if he were a god, and he kept squirming until he ended up on the man's lap.

"He really needs a nap," Toby repeated.

The man smiled. "He's okay, Toby, relax." Then he explained to a wide-eyed Max how planes worked.

Looking for something to do, Toby pulled down his tray, then returned it. He stared straight ahead, half-listening to the conversation. He wished the plane would suddenly fill with smoke; he wished he had gotten a drink so he could accidentally spill it. But nothing happened. No emergencies, no sounds, except the whoosh of the plane as it glided above the hills and valleys below.

RICH GIRL

▶ ▶ ▶ ▶ ▶

ONCE UPON A TIME I dated a rich girl from North Buffalo. One evening we were sitting in a love seat on her patio, watching her parents sip after dinner drinks in their living room. The backyard lawn was expertly groomed, plush, as if her father had hired the golf course landscaper to recreate the fairway on the club's first hole. Illuminated by large overhead lights, it seemed to glimmer, discouraging anyone from walking on it. It had been a clear, August night when we first sat down, but a light fog was coming in, dampening us. When I asked her to go inside to find a blanket, she disappeared around front.

This woman was a little crazy, but in an interesting way. One time she accused me of sleeping with her sister. She shoved me around her bedroom, knocking a framed poster of Courtney Love off the wall, cursing my inferior breeding, then trying to burn my face with her lit cigarette. Eventually, she stubbed it out on her forearm, its red eye disappearing into her soft white flesh. She never even blinked, just stared at me, her eyes slightly watering. I finally escaped from the bedroom, but got only halfway downstairs before her bony fist parted my shoulder blades, making me tumble five feet onto the hard living-room floor. I couldn't swing a club for two weeks. Another time, I watched her steal an Aerosmith CD from

Borders, stuffing it down the seat of her pants, so that you could see its rectangular outline as she strolled out. She wanted to get caught, and even though the alarm sounded and I saw the manager look directly at her ass—who wouldn't?—he let her go. Had he recently been the recipient of her affections? It was an interesting concept.

She was also the most beautiful girl I've ever slept with—straight blond hair down to her ass, perfect teeth, and a walk, which was both arrogant and sexy. When I made love to this woman, I never said, "I love you." I wasn't going to find my soul mate here. I was obsessed by the power in her hips, her parents' power, the knowledge that she would always be taken care of—moved from college to college when she flunked out, or sent off to an obscure Caribbean island if she hooked up with the wrong guy. One night when her father's Jag broke down outside a restaurant in Batavia, I suggested we take the bus back to Buffalo. She laughed and called a cab. She charged it to her father, and I remember thinking I could've bought a new set of Pings with that cab fare.

When she returned with the blanket, she sat next to me and draped it over our laps. She slid her legs under her ass and nuzzled her cheek against my chest. I handed her rum and Coke to her and breathed the clean scent of her hair. From my vantage point, I could see her parents: her mother reading a magazine, her father stretched out on the couch, newspaper in one hand, a gin and tonic in the other. The news was on, and when Tom Brokaw's face filled the screen, their daughter's head disappeared underneath the blanket. I grabbed her drink to make things easier, and there I sat in a kind of sexual twilight zone: two rum and Cokes in hand, the fog thickening, a warmth spreading across my thighs, so relaxed that our drinks nearly slid out of my hands. As I tightened my grip around the glasses, an enormous moth appeared about four inches from my face. It darted back and forth a few times, crashing clumsily into my nose. Startled, I spilled some of the drinks onto the blanket, hearing a muffled laugh below.

Maybe my sudden jerk attracted his attention, or perhaps he was just stretching, or maybe he felt some paternal tug in his middle-aged loins, but, whatever the case, he lowered his newspaper and glanced at me. He squinted and waved. Then I saw her mother, not smiling, not frowning, but displaying that superior, dispassionate glare she often turned my way. Looking back at them, I tried to see myself through their eyes: a possible son-in-law, slowly disappearing in the fog, sitting on a love seat with a blanket over his waist, a drink in each hand, with the kind of smile only fellatio could stir.

Her father relinquished his drink and shrugged his shoulders. He laughed and spread his hands questioningly; he was inquiring about the location of his daughter. I smiled, slowly waving my arms, trying not to spill the drinks or to disturb her for fear she'd come popping up like an out-of-breath snorkeler. He laughed again, and so did I, as if we had some good-old-boy conspiracy going. Then he stood and walked toward the glass doors.

I tried to alert her, I really did, but she must have interpreted my movement as a sign of pleasure. I kept waving my arms, gesturing him back, but he came forward until it appeared as if he'd been shot in the back by some bolt of wisdom. He quickly turned and walked away. He had no other option unless he was ready to accept that his daughter was going down on the local golf pro within pitching-wedge distance of him. After that night, he never spoke to me again, which was too bad because I know he liked me. He often praised my putting and said I was fun to have at parties.

Later, when I explained the incident to his daughter, she laughed, and for the rest of the night she was very seductive. We ended up at her friend's apartment on the West Side, where we made love three times, and if she had whispered "Daddy" into my ear after each one, I wouldn't have been surprised.

A TRADITION

EARL STARKS WAS a gentle father, an understanding father, yet, like many fathers in his neighborhood, he was often annoyed by his son's performance on the baseball field. He himself had been a good athlete, one of those kids who stayed after practice and ran extra laps, who carried the coach's bat and ball bag not because he was an ass-kisser but because he liked the feel of the canvas on his back, the weight of the equipment. He was the kind of kid who'd go to sleep with his mitt under his pillow or walk the halls of his school squeezing a rubber ball in his pitching hand. But, unfortunately, he couldn't handle pressure. He'd always strike out to end a possible big inning, or mishandle what could have been the final ground ball of a playoff game. And when he first sensed this same weakness in his son Billy, he decided that if he couldn't cure himself, he was going to at least save Billy.

In fact, Billy was a very talented ballplayer, but, unlike Earl, he didn't love or respect the game. And it wasn't as if Earl hadn't tried. Every year he bought season tickets to the Buffalo Bisons, even pulling Billy out of school for a few games. He sent him to baseball camps at local colleges and spent hundreds of dollars on private instruction. He bought him the best bats and gloves, and when Billy was nine years old, Earl took him to Cooperstown where they argued all day.

Billy couldn't have cared less about Ty Cobb's uniform or the plaques of famous ballplayers lining the walls. Instead, he wanted to visit the Corvette Museum, ride go-carts, and eat doughboys. Still, Earl had harbored hope for this spring because Billy was starting Little League, and how could a kid, especially one with Billy's talent, not be in awe of the possibilities? But little had changed. Earl still had to force him to hit practice balls off the batting tee, and he still had to yell at him when he goofed around on the bench. Billy didn't even appreciate that Earl had agreed to be an assistant coach, a position he was forced into when the other fathers couldn't find the time, and when they discovered that Luther Rumble, an off-and-on again handyman and notorious pot smoker, had somehow become head coach.

Luther. He of the blue hair. Luther. Forty pounds overweight, single, and knowledgeable of every X-rated Internet site, with a seemingly inexhaustible supply of dirty white T-shirts with "Bite Me" emblazoned on the front. He even had one with "Pulp Friction" etched in red—a not-so-subtle advertisement for a local strip joint. An embarrassment, for sure, yet the only adult male who promised to be at every practice and every game. He may have been stoned at a few of them, but at least he was there, pressing his heel into a player's back when he tried to raise himself at the end of a pushup drill, or mercilessly smashing a batting helmet when another player dropped a pop fly. Earl thought Luther was a thug, certainly not a professional like himself, yet he had to respect him for putting in the time.

Unfortunately, Luther didn't feel the same way about Earl. Earl could still remember that first practice in mid-April, a damp Saturday morning, the ground still hard from an early spring cold spell. The day started out badly with Earl trying at least four times to wake up Billy. It was the same ritual as last year. Earl would open Billy's bedroom door, and Billy would wrap a pillow around his ears, pleading exhaustion. "Excuses are for losers!" Earl would say, mimicking a bumper sticker he had forced Billy to tape over his bed. "I'll bet the rest of the kids are up."

Billy would counter with, "The rest of the kids care less than me." Then Earl would say, "I've made a commitment to this team, you know," which usually made Billy crawl out from under the covers.

But that day Earl's big concern was the weather. He thought it was too cold and damp to begin the season, and he felt sure Luther would cancel practice. All morning he had tried to call him but couldn't get through. Earl could picture Luther, eyes bloodshot, fingers stained with weed, zapping up pictures hot enough to melt his computer screen. Earl was so sure practice would be canceled that when he woke up he put on some new chinos, a crew neck sweater over a polo shirt, and his topsiders. Certainly, after Luther sent everyone home, Earl could stop by the office and clean up some paper work. He became even more sure of his plan when it began to rain heavily.

When he and Billy arrived at practice, Earl noticed patches of water around the mound and home plate and a few large puddles on the base paths. All the cars were lined up, all the fathers alive with anticipation, all the sons nodding off—everyone waiting for Luther to pull up in his burgundy Lincoln Continental. When the car finally arrived, the trunk and the driver's door simultaneously opened, and Luther appeared on the sidewalk. Earl stepped out of his Volvo to greet Luther, who grunted a few times, then tossed a large canvas bag of equipment onto the wet ground. He eyed Earl up and down, seemingly amused, then said, "Grab the batting tee, Starks, and get those lazy twerps out of their cars."

It was a long morning, everyone soaking wet, falling down, throwing errant pitches. Luther finished up practice with a sliding drill where the boys had to run from second base and slide head-first into the muddy area around third. When they complained, he said they could quit if they didn't like it. Surprisingly to Earl, many of the fathers who had remained at practice and were gathered behind the backstop taunted their uncooperative sons, calling them "babies" and "sissy girls." During all this name-calling, Earl stood in the cool mist, freezing and hatless.

To make matters worse, he had completely destroyed his chinos and topsiders. At one point, when he sat down on a wet bench, trying to wipe off some mud, Luther called him "GQ" for the first time. "GQ," he laughed, "forget about those shoes and pitch some batting practice." For a moment, all the fathers and sons froze, wondering what Earl would do. Earl knew that if he was going to make a stand, now was the right time, but he didn't say anything.

First, he was confused because the other fathers were supporting Luther's tough-guy approach to their sons; secondly, he sensed that old fear creep back into his chest, that old tightness in his back and neck; and thirdly, he knew that if you pissed off the coach, your son wouldn't play, even if you were one of the assistant coaches.

Consequently, he begrudgingly accepted the tag "GQ." Sometimes a few players murmured it when they thought Earl was pushing them too hard, or Earl would hear the nickname rise above a huddle of boys as they awaited practice fly balls. But what really bothered Earl was that Billy was too insecure to tell the boys to shut up. It was that weakness again, that sick gene, taking on a new form. In Earl's mind, it was precisely this insecurity that kept Billy from being a winner and a leader.

"You can't hesitate when you have a baseball coming at you at sixty miles per hour," he would tell Billy. "You need to be confident. You have to pound the ball."

In short, Earl wanted a son with guts, someone the other kids would look up to, though he didn't want to be another Jack Spencer. Just last week, after his son Jamie had struck out, Jack had taunted him as he walked back to the bench. At another game, when Jamie had dropped a pop up, Jack ran onto the field and began to spank him, dragging him off to his pickup. Earl had almost intervened, but then he remembered another rule of baseball: you don't tell a father how to speak to his son.

Unlike Spencer, Earl had decided to try a more practical and mature way to motivate Billy. He had bought tapes on hitting, fielding, and pitching, and, at least twice a week, he watched them with Billy, periodically quizzing him. He even typed a checklist of five major points that Billy was supposed to review before he came to the plate:

1) Watch the pitcher. Does he a throw a fastball on the first pitch? Does he throw a strike?

2) Get a comfortable batting position.

3) Relax your shoulders.

4) Take a deep breath.

5) And NEVER wiggle the bat.

Earl thought these were simple rules any moron could follow, so he felt justified when he yelled at Billy for wiggling the bat. Was he just supposed to let him strike out? "Take responsibility for yourself," he kept yelling at him on the way home after one of Billy's mediocre performances.

Billy blamed the umpire, said he didn't really care if he played baseball, then finally complained that he had a sore throat. But Earl would have none of it. "I go to work when I don't feel well," he yelled. Then he called Billy a "loser," so loudly and for so long that Billy began to cry and shake, and Earl, who felt as if his head were going to explode, almost drove them into a telephone pole. Earl didn't sleep too well that night. He felt as if he had a baseball stuck in the middle of his chest, and he swore that he'd never lose control again.

As he and Billy were reviewing tapes on hitting a few nights before the championship game, Earl thought about this incident. He stared at Billy, who looked as if he'd rather be watching reruns of "Saved By the Bell," and he angrily fast-forwarded to the sequence on balance. For the last few games Billy was popping up everything because he didn't have his weight evenly distributed.

Earl stopped the tape and stood in front of the TV. "Watch me," he said. "It's like the guy says. Spread your legs, then crouch and let your hands touch the ground. Now you're ready to grab the bat."

Billy was looking in a different direction, fiddling with a large candle on the end table.

"Are you listening?" Earl said.

"We've already been through this," Billy said. "Last week it was my grip, the week before my wiggle. Maybe I just stink."

"But you're a natural," Earl insisted. "You just have to follow the checklist. You can be one of the best hitters in town."

"If I'm a natural, why should I follow a checklist? Shouldn't it all come 'naturally'?"

"You know what I'm talking about."

"But I don't feel like a natural," Billy said. "I don't even know if I care anymore."

"Jesus Christ," Earl said, tossing the TV controls onto the couch.

Then his wife, who, obviously, had been listening to their conversation, came out from the kitchen. "He's just a boy," she said. "It's only a game."

Instead of replying, Earl disappeared upstairs into his study. Only a game? he thought. No, it was more than that. It was about excelling, commitment, integrity, responsibility.

The next morning, at the breakfast table, Billy acted as if nothing had happened. He even said he was going to have a big game. But his feeble attempt at confidence couldn't settle the queasiness in Earl's stomach. He almost wished that Billy would trip and break an ankle, so that he wouldn't be able to lose the biggest game of the year. This feeling followed him through his day at work and also at practice, where he could sense an increased tension in the other fathers.

The ones whose sons were starters said, "Well, whatever happens, happens," knowing fully well that if the team lost they would be tormenting their sons for weeks.

Those who were afraid their sons would choke took another tack. Anticipating failure, they said, "Even if the team loses, I can't complain. My son had a good year."

Then there were the remaining fathers who were angry that their sons didn't start or were forced to play behind weaker players. Matt Farley was one of these fathers. His son had more experience at third base than Billy, yet he only played when Billy was sick or forced to pitch. And every time Billy would make an error or strike out, Earl could sense Farley smirking at him. Which, in turn, made Earl harder on Billy. "What do you think it's like seeing

Matt Farley?" he had complained just yesterday. "Do you see how your failures affect me?"

"Why do you care what Farley thinks?" Billy had responded. It was a question Earl couldn't quite answer.

At practice the day before the big game, Farley showed up, pacing around the baseball field. Earl seemed to see him every time he looked up. He even thought Farley deliberately brushed against him when walking to the Porta-Potty. And during a break in practice, Farley came over and talked to Earl about the new sewage treatment plant and about the Red Sox. Then he mentioned the big game. "I think Billy's going to have a big day," he said. "He's really overdue."

Earl took the bait, admitting that Billy wasn't having one of his better years. Farley just said, "Well, it doesn't matter what you did last year. That's what I tell my kid."

By the time Earl realized he'd been set up, the break was over and Luther was screaming for everyone to do laps. As the players were running, Luther pointed at Spencer and said, "That fuckhead giving you a tough time?"

"It's nothing," Earl replied. "And please don't use the F-word around the kids."

Luther laughed. "I don't hear them complaining."

"That's because they're kids."

"GQ," Luther said, "let me explain something about me and the F-word. It's my favorite word. I use it as a noun, like in 'Don't look at my girlfriend like that, you dumb fuck.' I use it as an adjective, like in 'Will you throw a fuckin' strike, Billy?' And I use it as a verb, like in 'My assistant coach Starks is fuckin' with my head with his F-word problem.'" He laughed loudly and slapped Earl on the back.

Earl was going to respond, but realized it would do no

good. He just wanted practice to end, so he could get home and mentally prepare Billy for the game.

The next day Earl had trouble concentrating at work. He misplaced a brief and was fifteen minutes late for a court appointment. Then he realized that he had left his lunch at home, so he stopped at a nearby sandwich shop for a meatball sub, which lay at the bottom of his stomach like a bag of sand. When he finally did get home, his wife told him there was a message from Luther. "Please don't get upset," she said.

"What happened?" he asked.

"Just check the message."

Earl pressed the answering machine button and heard Luther's voice. "A bad day here, Starks. I fell off a fuckin' ladder and broke my foot. Probably won't make it to the game. Good luck, GQ."

That was it. No directions. No suggestions. Nothing. Earl felt a wave of panic, and, for over an hour, he tried unsuccessfully to reach Luther. He wanted to know who was pitching and what the batting order was. He even drove by Luther's house, but no one was there, and when he got home, he developed a bad case of diarrhea. About an hour later, Billy came home and Earl told him about Luther.

"I think we'll have a better chance of winning now," Billy said, "and I won't have to watch you swallow any more of Luther's crap."

It was a nice sentiment, but Earl hardly heard it. His heart was racing; every muscle in his body hurt. He thought of faking a fainting spell, but he knew Billy would suspect something. He also remembered the big words he'd been throwing around: excellence, responsibility, integrity. Fucking Luther, he thought.

When they arrived at the ballpark, the other team was

warming up, and there were a number of fathers waiting for Earl. A few of them seemed mad because he was late and hadn't taken the field first. Jack Spencer confronted him, yelling that "IT" was all about intimidation, warning Earl that the other coach, an angry, red-headed Irish guy named Crotty, was a master of "IT."

"You should have been here a half hour earlier," Spencer said, walking disgustedly away, "a half hour earlier." Earl was going to tell Spencer that it would have been difficult to take the field without any bats or balls, but he knew it wouldn't have registered in Spencer's little mind, made even smaller by the tension of the impending game. But Earl also sensed that there was something else bothering Spencer. "Everyone has to suck it up today," he boomed, looking as if his fat red face was going to pop off his shoulders.

Turning from Spencer, Earl looked around him. Most of the fathers were sitting in the bleachers, nervously waiting for the equipment to show up. Behind the backstop, Jess Prosser was squatting quietly with his son, Tom, who himself was meditating on a brand-new baseball resting on his lap. Jess, an aging hippie, believed that his son would focus better if before each game he had some quiet time with a baseball.

Off to the right of Jess, another player, Rick Sweeney, was hitting soft-tosses from his father, Ben, into a rusty old wire-mesh fence. "Keep your head down," Ben yelled. "Hold the bat up high. No, no, you have to shift your weight and break your wrists." Rick, a short fat boy, seemed confused but kept swinging, trying as best he could to please his father. "Jesus Christ, if you'd just lose some weight," Ben said, going nose-to-nose with Rick, screaming, "As in, don't eat."

Things were getting ugly when the big burgundy

Lincoln Continental pulled up, and Luther stepped out in uniform and not wearing a cast.

"I thought you broke your foot," Earl said.

"Don't wet your pants, GQ," Luther laughed. "It was just a sprain. I ain't going nowhere." He walked away and greeted the other fathers, who, to Earl's surprise, seemed happy he was there. Crotty still had his team on the field, pretending not to notice Luther's arrival.

"Get those pansies off the field," Luther yelled, and everyone laughed, then he announced positions, and Earl's heart sank when Billy wasn't assigned to third. How could he not start Billy today? But then Luther said, "Billy, go warm up. You're pitching."

Earl flinched, thinking what Billy was probably thinking: Why wasn't Jamie Spencer pitching? More important, Earl was upset because he hadn't had time to prepare Billy. They could have studied pitching tapes last night; Earl could have made a new checklist.

His thoughts were interrupted when Luther said, "GQ, are you going to hit ground balls or what?" After the warm-up, Earl asked Luther why Billy was pitching. "Spencer said his kid's arm's hurting. What's your problem?"

Which was a good question since most of the fathers would have wanted their sons to pitch this game. No doubt, Spencer had been spending most of the previous night calling his son a "sissy" and a "puke" for not fighting through the pain. But Earl was afraid that in a game as important as this one, Billy would get wild early, walk everyone, and all the fathers would see him blow the game. He could point out to Billy that he was dropping his shoulder, or not pushing off with his back leg, or not following through, but it wouldn't matter. Earl's face was tingling. He walked over to Billy and told the catcher to go back to the bench. "You feeling okay?" he asked.

"I'm fine."

"You sure."

"Yeah, I'm fine," he said.

But Earl was only half-listening, too busy mentally inventing a checklist. He caught about ten of Billy's warm-up pitches, until he heard Luther yell, "GQ, get over here. Don't pitch the kid out."

As Earl walked back to the bench, he saw Billy shaking his head. The stands behind the bench were loaded with fathers. Some were talking casually to each other, others yelling out encouragement to their sons, a few looking comatose, made frigid by the big game.

Luther addressed the players. "Okay, dickweeds. Personally, I don't care if we win or lose, but if anyone quits on me, and that includes you, Billy, I'll take away your *Playboys*."

All of the fathers laughed, but Earl was angry that Luther had singled out Billy, and on his way to get a drink of water, he told him so. "I don't know who's a bigger sissy," Luther replied. "You or your kid."

"You're an asshole, Luther," is all Earl could say.

The first five innings were scoreless, but in the bottom of the sixth, Earl's team scored first. The center fielder, Joe Marbury, walked and stole second. Then Tom Prosser surprised everyone by lining a double to left field, which scored Marbury. When Tom reached second, he placed his hands together and bowed in the direction of left field. "What a screwball," Luther said.

During those six innings, although Billy didn't strike out many batters, he held his own, and his team made superb defensive plays. But in the top of the seventh, Earl could see the old nerves at work. The first batter lined hard to third, and Jamie Farley made a diving catch. "You show 'em," Matt Farley yelled from the bleachers. "Stick it to the coach," he added, being held back by two other fathers.

The next batter hit a deep drive to center, which Joe Marbury tracked down. Earl could feel the muscles in his neck tighten, a feeling that was justified when the next two batters singled, and Billy walked a third batter to load the bases. "Want me to talk to him?" he asked Luther.

"What's that going to do? Just throw a lousy strike," Luther yelled.

"Take him out, Luther," Jack Spencer screamed, tearing off his Buffalo Bisons hat and throwing it to the ground.

Luther looked toward Spencer and laughed.

Suddenly, Earl understood that, indeed, this game meant little to Luther, that he was going to let Billy finish the inning for reasons of his own. It was as if he were enjoying everyone's discomfort, which became more severe when Billy threw three bad pitches to the next batter, the last one bouncing in front of the plate, nearly getting past the catcher.

"Take a deep breath," Earl yelled, and Luther laughed again. Billy scowled at Luther, kicking the dirt on the mound.

"I think he just said the F-word," Luther laughed. But Earl was paying attention to the game, watching as Billy's next pitch was driven deep over the left fielder's head—but foul.

"Jesus, Jesus, Jesus Christ," Jack Spencer yelled. "He's choking. Get him out of there."

Earl felt as if he could hear every derogatory comment from the bleachers, coupled with Luther's laughter and the screaming of Coach Crotty. He wanted to walk slowly to the mound and soothe Billy, but he also wanted to kick him in the ass; he wanted to tell him that this was one of those defining moments that could forever change his life. But anything Earl might have said would've been drowned out by the yelling around him. "Keep the game moving," the umpire yelled, as the catcher threw the ball back to Billy.

Billy took a deep breath and looked at Earl. He went into his motion and threw a high fastball. The batter swung hard, hitting a towering pop up just to the left of the mound. All the runners took off, and Jamie Farley called for the ball. But as he moved under it, his toe hit a bump in the infield, and he fell flat on his face. Noticing this, Billy dove, stretching out as far as he could. When the ball finally came down, it landed in the webbing of his mitt, and the game was over.

All the players rushed to the mound and lifted Billy onto their shoulders; all the fathers hugged each other, jumping up and down. Earl still hadn't moved, shocked that Billy had finally answered the challenge. He imagined a long line of future successes, and he knew the other fathers would envy him. Certainly, this past year had been a struggle, but all the hard work and badgering had paid off. Earl was proud of Billy, and also of himself, and as he ran towards the mob forming on the mound, he hoped that the fathers and sons would lift him onto their shoulders, too. After all, he was one who had worked so hard with Billy. Surely, this was his day, too, one that both he and Billy would remember for the rest of their lives.

EX-RAY

"OH, JUNEY JUNE, be my girl and your Daddy'll do right by you," is what Ray told me to say, thinking she wanted a homeboy but knowing she'd end up with Denzel Washington instead. Which made us laugh as we drove down the New York State Thruway somewhere between Buffalo and Syracuse, one minute on dry pavement, the next the sky exploding, a million white fireflies raining down upon us, Ray crouched over the wheel, opening the window, popping the wipers clean, over and over, trying to keep the tires in the narrow ruts, me too stoned on Xanax to help, thinking there's nothing like this in Rhode Island, nothing ever. We're on the edge of the world for all we know, the radio blasting, Ray pleading, "Just wait a minute, Ex-Ray, just turn it down, man, I can't think, say your prayers, Ex-Ray, it's the cold hand of God come down to smite us."

Ray is beautiful. Ray is strong and smart. Ray is cool and contained. Ray taught me how to swing a hammer, how to paint a basement, how to tie a wet bandanna around my head when the sun gets hot. He taught me how to terrify a foreman with a nail gun, then drop-kick that same foreman off a subfloor and lose my job, because from the moment I met Ray, I was going where he went, and though Ray did the actual kicking, I was in that kick, too, pissed at every guy who pulled rank on me, who pushed me, who knew I had no father to teach me how to live. And though I know I can never be Ray, I can still be Ex-Ray.

One night me and this white guy go to a hockey game, and I'm feeling odd, shapes clearly outlined, everyone fitting neatly into them. Later at a bar, we're playing pool, click, click, click, everything falling into place, balls dropping into leather pockets with a sense of urgency. But then a strange and sad dizziness. I'm waiting for I'm not sure what, but I know a question's being asked, know there's an answer, very close, too, but I'm unable to glimpse it, even when I'm back home, lighting a cigarette, contemplating the curved neck of that question, staring out the living-room window, the rain coming down, the neighborhood asleep, my mom asleep, my dad dead long ago, rain peppering the road, the front lawn spotted with puddles, telephone lines humped with beads of water. Then Silence, heavy with rain—inviting, bottomless Silence—suddenly comes forth, and I embrace it, being in the question like in a huge prehistoric egg, terrified from that day forth.

I'm waiting for Ray's call, halving my pills with a Swiss Army knife. I put one in my shirt pocket, another in the watch pocket of my jeans in case the old dread arrives, whereupon I'll swallow and forget for a while, sometimes even becoming Ray, who right now is telling me I don't have to drive. He says Linda told him to get another job or she'll leave, that she wants to get married and have a kid. Then I hear a click, then a honk outside, so I take another half and one more. I stumble downstairs, grabbing the railing, hugging the wall, my mom in her chair, asleep, the newspaper draped over her chest like a bib. Her mouth's half-opened as if practicing for death. Does she know my real parents speak to me? Does she know what I'm capable of, that I stiffen when I think of these things, as if God Himself reaches into my heart and says, "Ex-Ray, that sleeping woman saved you from your Black junkie parents," because only He can see that black boat anchored in my head, its captain, shotgun in hand, standing on its prow.

If my mom were to change into something, she'd be a large boulder, sanded smooth by years of wind and rain, and I'd paint a large heart on it with red paint.

We're in Linda's car, a brand-new red Ford Escort station wagon. The day she bought it Ray asks, "You going upscale on me?" And Linda asks back, "What's upscale about an Escort?" Then Ray says, "Next, you'll be sleeping with a lawyer." Then Linda says, "Only if he gives back rubs like you, Ray." And that's how they get along, but not tonight, just Ray saying, "Ex-Ray, we're on our way." "To where?" I ask. "To some other planet," he says, giving that Ray-laugh, full of confidence and trouble, mostly because of the Jack Daniel's wedged between his seat and emergency brake on this mid-January night, roads as crystal clear as Ray's question: "You with me, Ex-Ray? You thought about it, man? Because this car has a mind of its own." I'm hoping he's right. I'm hoping he's wrong.

If Linda were to change into something she'd be a swan, or a lilac bush, and I'd place her flowers in a jar next to my bed, and I'd never tell Ray.

Juney June is June, Alice is Christine, women we met at Louie's the night Ray named them, just like he named me—all of us actors in a movie written by yours truly, Ex-Ray.

Cast of Characters

RAY: About six feet four inches tall. Very handsome. Strong. Irish, light brown hair tied back into a ponytail, green eyes, and a square jaw. Always wears blue jeans and untied work boots. Always wears flannel shirts. Often agitated.

ALICE, a.k.a. Christine: About five feet tall. Short red hair, cut like Cleopatra's, bright red lipstick, a red butterfly-shaped birthmark on her left cheek. A little chunky. Knee-high brown leather boots with zippers. When she sits on a barstool and crosses her legs, you can see she doesn't wear panties. Very often complains.

JUNE, a.k.a. Juney June, a.k.a. Ex-Ray's Juney June: Also about five feet tall, very thin. Short, purple hair spiked in sections. Tight blue T-shirt, tight black stretch pants, black high heels. Angelic.

EX-RAY: A Black guy. Our Hero. Usually nervous.

ALICE: [*sipping a White Russian*]: I don't want to be called Alice.

JUNEY JUNE: [*sitting on a stool, hands between her legs*]: I like Juney June, it sounds like a bird's song or a new kind of print dress.

RAY: We should go someplace. We should run off and get married.

ALICE: You really are nuts.
RAY: [*leaning over and blowing into her ear*]: And you really are sexy.
ALICE: You going to keep calling me Alice?
RAY: When I saw you drinking that milkshake, I was going to call you Maalox.

[*Alice laughs*]

EX-RAY, OUR HERO [*talking to himself*]: Ray, if I could just be like you for a moment.
RAY: What was that Ex-Ray?
EX-RAY: Nothin', Ray.
JUNEY JUNE [*to Ex-Ray*]: Do you like Spike Lee?
EX-RAY: He's okay.
JUNEY JUNE: I've liked all his movies, but I thought everyone did all the wrong things in *Do the Right Thing*. I always say that and everyone laughs. Why didn't you laugh Ex-Ray?

[*Ex-Ray laughs, fingering a tiny, white pill in his watch pocket*].

RAY: Ex-Ray, stop playing with yourself!

[*Ex-Ray removes his hand from his pocket and waits for laughter to fade*].

ALICE: I want to know why you call him Ex-Ray.
RAY: We got drunk one night and decided to give each other nicknames, and because he's the dark side of me, like my alter ego, I named him Ex-Ray, with an Ex, not an X. [*Ray draws an X in the air*].
JUNEY JUNE: Like cutting your fingers and becoming blood brothers. That's cool.
RAY: Yeah, something like that. You know, you think like a poet.
EX-RAY: [*Talking to himself*]. You already have Alice, Ray, and Linda's at home. Let me have Juney June.
RAY: Stop mumbling, Ex-Ray. They're going to think

you're weird.
JUNEY JUNE: I don't think he's weird.
ALICE [*to Ray*]: So what's your nickname, Big Shot?
RAY: We couldn't come up with one. I guess I'm too big of a personality.
ALICE: No doubt.

[*Juney June and Ex-Ray go off to play a video game, which they never get to because Juney June keeps asking questions about being Black, which Ex-Ray has no answers to since he gets most of his information on this subject from books or TV, and he's more interested in just getting through the day without hurting himself or someone else*].

JUNEY JUNE: You should go to college, Ex-Ray. Anybody can go to a community college. I'm there now, taking this course called Genealogy, where you look up your family tree. I found out my family's from the same area as Tom Sawyer, so I'm thinking we might be related. Don't you ever want to look for your family tree?
EX-RAY: No, not really, but I'm glad you like me instead of Ray.
JUNEY JUNE [*laughing*]: What an odd thing to say, Ex-Ray.

[*Ex-Ray and Juney June go back to the bar where Alice is showing Ray some postcards].*

JUNEY JUNE: I was just asking Ex-Ray if he ever wanted to look into his family tree.
RAY: If Ex-Ray has a family tree, it probably has a noose with his neck size hanging from one of its branches.
EX-RAY *[trying to change the subject]*: Juney June says she thinks she's related to Tom Sawyer.
RAY: I thought he was a character in a book.
ALICE: A character in a book? You mean all this time you've been telling people you're related to someone in a book? That's as stupid as being related to cartoon characters.

[If Alice were to change into something, she'd be a weed or a plant with a big mouth, like a Venus' flytrap.]
EX-RAY [*coming to the rescue*]: A lot of characters in books are based on real people. I think that's what Juney June meant.
RAY: Yeah, that's right. I was probably wrong, anyway. I don't read books. [*He grabs Ex-Ray by the arm and pulls him close*]. Dig these postcards, Ex-Ray. Pictures of Niagara Falls in winter. Alice has this friend that moved there a month ago. Hardly anyone goes there in winter. Look what she writes on the back, "We want to see you, Alice, just show up." Just show up, Ex-Ray. What do you think about that?
EX-RAY: I think you should bring Linda's car home.
ALICE: Who's Linda?
RAY: My sister.
ALICE: Won't she mind?
RAY: Not Linda, she's a good egg.
JUNEY JUNE: I certainly want to go. What do you think, Christine? I mean Alice.
ALICE: I think it's a long way to go to get laid.
[*Ex-Ray sighs, then feels in his jacket pocket for his bottle of pills.*]

If Ray were to change into something, he'd be a big stray dog, like an Irish setter, and he'd love and protect you, then one day disappear like he never existed.

All four of us crammed into a Ford Escort station wagon on the New York State Thruway for nine hours in the middle of the night. Why didn't we count on the booze wearing off, or on Alice's boots, or on her saying, "I gotta pee again," or "Don't they have liquor stores on this road?" or "Why the hell did you have to finish the whole bottle of JD?" or "What are you doing, June, going down on him?" and finally, "If you call me Alice one more time, I'm going to punch you." All this for nine hours, her head one time vanishing into Ray's lap, but mostly just zipping and unzipping her leather boots, driving Ray a little bit crazy, until she says, "Did I tell you I slept with a guy who slept with Elton John," which is when Ray veers into a rest stop outside of Syracuse. "It's coffee time," he says, but we all see him making a phone call before he returns with the drinks. "Who the hell did you call?" Alice asks. "Linda," Ray replies. "You mean your sister?" Alice asks. "No," Ray says, "I mean the woman I'm living with."

Ex-Ray duly notes the following facts:

1. Alice punches Ray in the arm and says, "You think you can treat us like whores?"

2. Ray says, "What a mouth."

3. Alice says, "You weren't complaining about it an hour ago."

4. It begins to snow outside Ex-Ray's window, big wet flakes.

5. Juney June, who had fallen asleep on Ex-Ray's lap, awakens. Ex-Ray places his finger over her lips, saying, "Shhhh. . ."

Three hours of silence between Syracuse and Buffalo suggests that Ray and Ex-Ray will be alone in Niagara Falls.

Niagara Falls! My last image of Alice and Juney June—standing next to each other in front of a convenience store, Alice asking me to roll down my window, jamming her head into its opening. "You want a nickname, Big Shot?" she yells at Ray. "How about 'Jerk,' 'Asshole,' or 'Little Dick.'" As she starts to walk way, I roll up the window, but she turns as if she's forgotten something. She wheels around and hikes up her skirt, then presses her bare ass against the glass. A big laugh, then she turns and faces me. "This has nothing to do with you, Ex-Ray," she says. "You're cool." As Ray pulls away, I see Juney June for the last time. She's smiling, shrugging her small shoulders.

When Ray and I arrive at the American side of the Falls, the ground is snow-covered, the sky clear, the temperature feeling like zero. On the road to the tourist center something remarkable happens. Though we can't see the Falls, the mist is everywhere, and the trees seem made of glass, their branches and boughs encased in fine tubes of ice that shimmer beneath the sun. "It's like we're in one of those glass paperweights," I say. "I told you it'd be worth it," Ray says. "Totally exquisite, man. If Linda were only here." When we reach the tourist center, we see one parked car but no people. The sidewalks haven't been sanded or salted, so we have to tiptoe to a rise overlooking the Falls. Ray goes first, grabbing my hand and pulling me with him. I feel myself go numb—not because of the rush of falling water, or the mist, or the noise, but the fear of tumbling into the gorge, which seems as wide as one hundred football fields and as long as the finger of God. There are ice-covered stairs winding their way down to a scenic overlook, which is rimmed by a tubular metal fence, but we're blocked from the stairs by a chain and a sign announcing this space is off-limits until spring. Ray smacks the sign with the palm of his hand and says, "Fuck that," dragging me down the stairs, gripping the icy railing. When we reach the bottom, we're both too afraid to approach the fence. "This is crazy," Ray says, letting go of my hand, trying to crawl back up the stairs. I cling to the railing, not saying anything, but knowing I can't let Ray get away, so I grab his legs, pulling him down the first few steps. He probably thinks I'm just afraid, not knowing it has come into my head to hurl us into the foamy, deafening noise below. He tries to calm me, then pushes me away, making us both slide toward the fence. When he realizes we may disappear under it, he punches me in the face, freeing himself from my grip. Then he slowly stands, managing to drag me across the ice to where we first started. "Ex-Ray," he yells, punching me again, "What the fuck are you doing?"

What was it all about? you are probably asking. It was about a secret. Almost a year ago, Ray and I killed a guy, though "killed" isn't the right word. We didn't beat up or shoot anyone, but the fact remains some guy is dead, and if it wasn't for us he'd be alive. We knew there was going to be a snowstorm when we got to Louie's that night, but Ray drank hard, anyway. As the snow fell, people began to leave early, but Ray had fought with Linda that night, so he wanted to keep drinking. It was midnight by the time Louie threw us out. I asked him to call a cab, but Ray told us both to "fuck off," and a few minutes later we were driving Linda's '91 Lincoln down the unplowed, deserted streets of Providence. In our defense, Ray wasn't driving fast, and he didn't fall asleep, and he was trying to be careful, and why would some guy be walking in the middle of the street at midnight during a snowstorm, anyway, but he was, and before we could see him, we hit him from behind, watching him fly into the air and hearing him tumble over the back of the car. Ray pulled over and said, "Jesus." Then he said, "Stay here," and got out of the car. I could barely see him drag the body over to the curb, propping it up against a telephone pole. When he returned, I asked if the guy was alive and he told me to shut up. When he started to pull away, I grabbed the wheel, and he said, "He's dead, man." "How can you be sure?" I asked. "You want to see for yourself?" But I shook my head, "No." We knew it was wrong, but we left anyway, drove until we came to a phone booth in front of a gas station. Ray told me to call the cops. He told me to say, "A dead guy is on the side of the road at Admiral and Charles." The next few days, the paper was full of the news. I learned that the guy had died of a broken neck. I learned all about him, how many kids he had, where he worked, where his wife worked, where he was going to be waked, and, like Ray, I waited every day for a squad car to pull up and take me away. But it never happened. I think about this dead guy every day and feel very sad, but I've also learned that, given enough time, a person can live with most anything. And though you could argue that it was Ray, not me, who killed the guy, as I said before, from the moment I met Ray, my fate was tied to his. Thus, on that one strange winter night, I became Ex-Ray long before Ray ever thought of the name.

THE CHAIR

▶ ▶ ▶ ▶ ▶

PAUL COULDN'T BELIEVE Alicia wouldn't sell the chair. It squatted in the living room—an ugly chair, faded, with blue imitation velvet, its back formed by two thin vertical panels of wood, which pinched the shoulder blades of any normal man. He never sat on it, neither did she; even Christopher opted for the floor when he watched TV. Christopher was the boy standing opposite the chair. His soccer shorts were too tight, and when he bent over to examine the merchandise, Paul jokingly pulled the elastic on his waistband.

"Who's taking me to the game?" Christopher asked.

"I am," Paul said.

"Paul is," his mother yelled from the kitchen. She came into the living room, lugging a rusty wok.

"You going to clean that first?" Paul asked.

"I didn't realize you wanted to be in charge."

"I was just asking," he said. He knew she was still mad from last night. But he was mad, too.

Christopher kept digging through the merchandise and came up with something white in his hand. "You're not selling this, are you?" It was a ceramic polar bear about the size of the boy's hand with an aluminum clip attached to its base. "My polar bear," he said.

"The polar bear you've never used?" she laughed. "The

one I found in the basement behind the oil burner?"

"It's symbolic," Christopher complained.

"Of what? Neglect?"

"Of my old school."

"You hated that school."

"But that's when Grandma bought it for me."

"Then it's symbolic of Grandma?"

"It's symbolic of something," Paul intervened. "You should be able to understand that."

"Just keep the bear," she told Christopher. "But remember, I said you could sell anything that was yours."

"I don't remember that," he said, looking hard at the bear, then searching for other things he might call his own.

"Will you carry this wok to the porch?" she asked Paul. "We have to start pricing. We didn't do anything last night."

Paul grabbed the wok. "That wasn't my fault." He passed the chair on the way out and felt like kicking his foot through the backrest. This chair, he thought. This stupid, old chair. Back in the kitchen, he started on her. "I want you to sell that chair. Why torture me with it?"

"Don't be silly."

"It makes you think of him, doesn't it?"

"That's bizarre."

"But it's true."

"Shhh. Christopher will hear you."

"Do you think of him when you touch it?"

"My God. Shhh."

"Do you?"

When the front door slammed, she turned on him. "See what you've done?"

"Just remember who stopped him from sleeping in the park where all of Christopher's friends could see him."

"I appreciate that, but he wasn't always crazy."

Paul didn't want to hear that story again. To him, the only important point was that he was the one raising Christopher; he was the one who gave up his bachelor's apartment on the West Side and moved to the suburbs; he was the one painting the house and cutting the lawn. Sometimes, he'd rather have been sipping a cappuccino in one of the coffee shops spotting the West Side, or just hanging out at the Albright-Knox Gallery. But he loved Alicia and he was trying to stand by her. He touched her arm. "Just hold me," he said, but she backed away.

He went into the living room and dragged the chair into the kitchen. He sat on it, the thin wooden panels persecuting his back. He asked her to sit on his lap, but she walked into the living room. "I'm sorry," he said, following her. "I'm sorry, but you're hurting me."

"Jesus," she said, returning to the kitchen. She dragged the chair back through the living room out onto the porch, and down the front steps, leaning it against the telephone pole in front of the house. He watched her from the window. He had won.

Back in the apartment, she said, "You sell it."

"But I'm taking Christopher to the soccer game."

"Then at least price it."

Later, he'd place a dollar sticker on that killer of a backrest, thinking it would be the first piece of furniture to go. But for now, he said, "I'm not threatened by him. I feel sorry for him."

"The only one I feel sorry for is myself," she said.

There were only three minutes remaining in the soccer game. Paul thought the garage sale would be over by now. He hoped some big fat slob of a woman had bought the chair, and he imagined it caving in like an old building when she sat down. He gathered up Christopher's hat and sweatshirt, which the boy had shed when the day had turned suddenly warm. A woman handed him Christopher's water bottle. "Don't forget this," she said. She was Christopher's Cubmaster, a next-door neighbor, a large, athletic woman with big white teeth, who stalked the sidelines with her husband. At one game Paul had had the sudden urge to wrestle her to the ground and feel her muscles.

"Thanks," he said.

"You're a wonderful man," the woman said. "I couldn't say that when my husband was here. Of course you know what I mean."

Before Paul had a chance to consider exactly what she meant, he noticed a dark figure emerge over the hill, crawling through a layer of raw, orange maple leaves about a hundred yards away. Paul reached for the woman who thought he was wonderful, but she was off arguing with a referee. He looked back toward the trees and watched as the figure—like a cockroach suddenly surprised by light—disappeared. Sweat shirt and water bottle in hand, Paul ran toward the woods, kicking up piles of dead leaves, reaching the parking lot just in time to see a little black Escort peel out. Then he heard a whistle and Christopher's breathless voice. "Where are you going?" he asked.

"Home," Paul said. "We're going home."

In the car, they didn't speak, but Paul could feel Christopher looking at him. "I saw him, too," Christopher said. "I think he just wanted to see me play."

Paul took a shortcut home, only to find the street blocked by a fire engine. He tried to back up, but the other cars had penned him in. He left the car and ran toward a fireman, who was helping to extinguish a huge pile of burning leaves. "I have to get through," Paul said, imagining Christopher's father wielding an ax, smashing all the goods except for that stupid, old chair.

"Just hold your horses, Homer," the fireman said. "We'll be on our way in a moment."

"You don't understand."

"I understand you're in a very big hurry."

"You stupid jerk," Paul said, running back to the car. He maneuvered his front bumper around the car in front of him, and spun out on the lawn across the street, racing right past the parked fire truck. Embarrassed, Christopher crouched below the passenger window.

"I think he just wanted to see me play," Christopher said.

"Don't, Christopher," Paul yelled. "Just don't."

Having dodged the fire truck, Paul raced down Union Road, rushing past Southgate Plaza and running the red light in front of a supermarket. He made a sharp left turn, then another one, rocketing onto their street. He stopped suddenly when he saw Christopher's father, a tall, thin, unshaven man, with unkempt, shoulder-length hair. The bottom of his soiled T-shirt nearly reached the fringe of his cut-off denim shorts, and he wore a beat-up pair of black canvas Converse sneakers over sockless feet. He was touching the chair, talking to Christopher's mother. A young woman stood nearby, scrutinizing the wok.

Paul parked the car, and Christopher jumped out and ran into the house.

"Christopher?" the man said quietly.

"You could get into trouble for being here," Paul yelled, stepping out of the car.

"It's okay, Paul. He's leaving."

"I can't leave," the man said. "I need to buy this chair." He put his hand on the backrest. "My chair."

"Not anymore," Paul said.

"I have the money. It's only a dollar."

"I've raised it to thirty dollars. Now you'll have to go."

The man looked plaintively at Christopher's mother.

"Just take the chair," she said. "Just go."

"No," Paul said.

"Why are you doing this?" she asked.

He moved aggressively toward the man. "Because he sneaks around. Because he watches us."

"I just need the chair," he said.

Paul grabbed the chair by one leg and started to drag it toward the house. "Sorry, it's not for sale. Go home and take your Lithium."

The young woman who had been examining the wok approached Paul. "I've been listening," she said. "Why don't you just sell him the chair?"

"We don't care what you think," Paul hissed. Shocked, the woman moved off toward her car.

"I won't leave without the chair," the man said, moving toward Paul.

Christopher's mother came in between them and grabbed the side of the chair, but Paul wouldn't let go. Then Christopher's father grabbed one of the legs, and all three of them tugged simultaneously, Paul eventually wrenching the chair free. He lifted it over his head, swinging it wildly, not quite sure what to do, but then he spotted the telephone pole. He crushed the chair against it so hard that one skinny leg was all that remained in his hand, and he brandished it at the intruder like a sword.

Christopher's father grabbed one of the other broken legs, and the two men faced each other, as if preparing to duel. But then he suddenly dropped his guard, staring hopelessly at the piece of wood, his eyes filling with tears. "Can I keep this?" he asked his wife.

"Just go, please."

"Can I just speak with him?" he said.

Enraged, Paul waved the wooden leg over his head, forcing his opponent to the corner and then down another street. "You crazy bastard," he yelled at the gaunt figure retreating on his heels. "I'll give you your chair, by God."

From the living room window, Christopher had witnessed the entire scene. He was holding the ceramic polar bear and his palm hurt from squeezing it so tightly. He watched his mother as she gathered shattered pieces of the chair. She started to cry, then disappeared around the corner in pursuit of the two men. Christopher abandoned the window and walked into the kitchen. He stood over the plastic garbage can, dropping the polar bear into it, watching the white figure fall to the bottom. As it landed, he heard a dull thud; then he walked out onto the front porch and sat on the steps. In the distance, he could hear yelling, and he wondered who would come home first.

TWO TREESOMES

WHEN STONY PULLED OUT of the cemetery onto Ridge Road, he slid the Subaru Forester into fourth instead of second gear; it bucked a few times, then stalled in the middle of the road. His mother, who was sitting next to him, gasped as a shiny black pickup truck, its chassis riding high above two oversized tires, squealed to a stop in front of them. The truck was so close that Stony could see the man behind the wheel. His large head was shaved and he had a silver ring the size of an Oreo dangling from his left ear. He was swearing at Stony, his meaty arms quivering with each obscenity. Stony's mother lowered her window and shouted, "Give it a rest, the kid just got his permit."

"Fuck you, lady," he yelled.

"Let it go, Mom," Stony said. "The guy's an asshole." But by the time he had finished his sentence, she was out of the car. She had been a track star in college and still ran and lifted, but Stony knew she was no match for the guy in the truck. He eyed his bag of golf clubs resting in the back seat, wondering if he could get his hands on one of the metal woods.

When he turned around, his mother was leering into the window of the pickup, standing with both hands on her hips. "Fuck you back," she said.

The guy looked startled for a minute, then laughed out loud. He wagged his tongue at her in a crude sexual way, backing up the truck and driving away.

"Did you see that?" she asked Stony when she returned to the car. "Did you see that? If I ever see you do that to a girl, Stony, you'll be sorry." Before Stony could respond, a car started honking behind them. "Just pull over to the curb," she said. "Everyone's in a big hurry today."

Stony was beginning to see this mishap as another bad omen. First, a visit to the cemetery to lay down flowers on his grandfather's grave, then the guy in the truck, and now he had to face his biggest test: playing golf with his father, whom he hadn't see in a month.

"Sorry, Mom," Stony said, navigating the car next to the curb, "but no one drives a standard anymore."

"That's because they're stupid and lazy like your father."

"I didn't even mention him," Stony responded defensively.

"But I read the subtext, didn't I, dear? Yes, your father has an automatic in that old rattrap. That's the good news. The bad news is he never sees you."

"Geez, Mom," is all Stony could say, knowing his father's car certainly wasn't a rattrap, but instead a mint-condition, blue 1984 Grand Marquis with leather seats and a thousand dollar stereo system, equipped with a special amplifier switch under the steering wheel.

Stony's mother finally composed herself, brushing some strands of brown hair from her forehead. Yesterday she'd had her hair cut short, and she still hadn't gotten used to the bangs. "Sorry," she said, resting her hand on his. "You know I want you to have fun with your father."

"I know," Stony said, pulling away from the curb and

driving toward the Basilica. When he reached it, he turned right on South Park, then left into the entrance of the glass-domed Botanical Gardens, finally veering right and gliding into the golf club's parking lot. His father was standing at the first tee, leaning against a red ball-washer and talking to some men. As everyone always mentioned, he was a good-looking man—blonde, slender, and still physically fit because, like his mother, he ran and worked out with weights. The pronounced muscles in his chest and arms made his white T-shirt cling tightly to him. There was something written on the shirt, but Stony couldn't make out the words as his father ran toward the car, excited.

"Oh, Christ," Stony's mother said.

"Let's not have any trouble," Stony pleaded.

"Just grab your clubs and switch seats," she said, "before he revs up his engine."

But it was too late. Stony's father was already at his mother's door, helping her out of the car. "Nice wheels, June," he said. "You've finally embraced yuppiedom."

She couldn't help but laugh. "Same old Arthur, a smile and a smart-ass comment for everyone. Nice T-shirt, too."

Stony could now read the green print on his father's chest: "South Buffalo Boys Do It Better."

"At least they got the 'boys' right," his mother said.

"Geez, Mom," Stony sighed, getting out of the car, hoping to grab his golf bag and escape into the clubhouse.

"Can't you see you're embarrassing the kid?" his father said.

She laughed and pushed by Stony's father, circling the car and jumping into the driver's seat. She started the engine and began to pull away. "Goodbye, sweetie," she said.

"Goodbye, sweetie," Stony's father replied, walking

behind the moving car. "And I like your hair. You look like a little gymnast."

Stony stood there with the weight of his bag on his shoulder. "I think she was talking to me," he said.

"Just having some fun, Stony. What's her problem?"

"We went to grandpa's grave, then almost had an accident."

"Why did you go to his grave?

"It's his birthday."

His father grimaced. "Stony," he said, "with all due respect for the dead, your grandfather was the man who destroyed my marriage. One day your mother realized she didn't marry her father, and it was all downhill from there."

Stony had heard this complaint before, so he didn't respond.

"I could tell you stories, Stony," but fortunately he decided not to. Instead, he grabbed Stony playfully by the arm and said, "God, you look great."

That was his father in a nutshell. Stony hadn't seen him in a month, which hurt him to the core, but then with a phrase or two, or a squeeze of an arm, Stony was five years old again, following him around the house like a little poodle.

"Let me take the bag," he said, grabbing it and walking toward the clubhouse. "We don't tee off for forty-five minutes. Let's get a Coke, and I'll show you off."

And that's what he did, stopping by tables and bragging about Stony's prowess on the baseball field, even though he had never been to a game, or praising his "A" average, even though he had never met one of Stony's teachers. But Stony still loved to hear his father go on. He loved to watch his body language, see that infectious smile. It was clear the men respected him.

Lately Stony hadn't played South Park, but instead frequented the private clubs where his school friends belonged. He almost laughed when over the entrance to the clubhouse he saw the new sign: "South Park Country Club." It was a short nine-hole course, with dirt instead of grass tees. Sometimes the tees were so hard you had to drive a nail into them to soften the dirt. And the holes were far from picturesque, landscaped around a stagnant pond where dead fish often floated.

To make things worse, the entire course was encircled by an asphalt road, on which teenagers raced each other in souped up late-model sports cars. South Park wasn't the kind of course where you would retrieve a ball after knocking it into the pond, and if you hooked or sliced a shot over the road (which wasn't hard to do because of the narrowness of the fairways), you had better forget it, unless you wanted to get run over. But in spite of its shortcomings, Stony had a soft spot for the course. This was where he had learned to play golf, and he liked to be around the working-class men in the clubhouse. Sometimes he was annoyed by their ideas, but he appreciated their sincerity. If they didn't like you, they said so, unlike at the private clubs where everyone was overly nice to each other. Stony also had good memories of the clubhouse, with its heavy wooden tables and its chairs with backs wrapped in cracked, dark red leather.

He remembered how in the summer he and his friends would get dropped off at 7 A.M. and picked up at 3 P.M. They'd play thirty-six holes a day and sip Cokes while eating their homemade peanut butter or baloney sandwiches. And Myron still worked the bar and grill, which was where he and his father drifted toward after making the rounds of three tables. Myron was an overweight, ex-railroad man with a cherubic face and one arm, having lost the other one under a wheel of a railroad car. He always wore a soiled white T-shirt, the sleeve of his absent arm rolled up and safety-pinned.

"Arthur and son," Myron laughed, when he saw them coming. He poured them some Cokes, then scanned a sheet listing the tee times. He shouted out to the whole club. "Listen up. Art's teeing off after the Serbs." Everyone laughed, including Stony's father. Stony had no idea what anyone was talking about, but he sensed that the "Serbs" were somehow going to be a part of his near future.

"Did your dad tell you about the Serbs, Stony?" Myron asked. He became suddenly serious, his face reddening with rage. "What's this club about?" he demanded.

Stony didn't know how to reply.

"Excuse him, Myron," his father laughed, "he goes to private school."

"Whose club is this?" Myron asked.

Stony shrugged his shoulders.

"Look around you," Myron directed him. "You've got Micks, Polaks, Krauts, Dagos." As he mentioned each ethnic group, men laughed and raised their hands, taking responsibility for their bloodlines.

Franklin Johnson and his brother Fred stood up. "You forgot the Negroes," Franklin said in mock seriousness, but Myron wasn't laughing.

"Yeah, yeah," he said, "Blacks, too." Then he turned to Stony again. "Do you know what the Serbs are doing over there? Your dad says you're a smart boy."

Stony knew something about Bosnia, but he was too busy with school and sports to read the papers. Suddenly, his father placed a hand on Stony's arm. He looked him in the eye. "They're killing people, Stony, and now they're coming over here. These are people we've never seen before, with a lot of money and time on their hands. They're ruining it for the good Serbs who've been here for years."

"Arrogant sons of bitches," Myron added, slapping a towel on the bar.

This kind of talk sounded bad to Stony. He had overheard it in the clubhouse since he was a kid. His father's friends would catch a scrap of current events or a political commentary on CNN, or they'd read an article in the Sunday paper and become instant authorities on everything from the Kennedys to mad cow disease. His father especially enjoyed these moral and intellectual rampages. His mother called it "mission talk." "Your father's off on another 'mission,'" she would say. Stony had even accompanied him on a few.

There was the time the heel from one of his new shoes came off, and when the shoe store wouldn't take them back, his father dragged him down to the mall where he held the store manager against a display window until the security guards arrived. Sometimes his missions seemed driven by a code of honor or a sense of honesty; other times his motive wasn't so clear, as was the case today.

"Sons of bitches, all of them," Myron repeated, and the heads at all the tables nodded in agreement. As they did, as if in synch with some bizarre script, six strangers tumbled through the clubhouse's screen door.

So these were the "Serbs," Stony thought, tracking everyone's reaction to their entrance. Stubbled-faced and dressed in what appeared to be second-hand polo shirts, faded jeans, and beat-up tennis shoes, they certainly didn't look that ominous or rich, except for one man who appeared to be their leader. Unnaturally thin, he had heavily-greased wavy black hair, chiseled features, and a tanned complexion. He wore a red flower-print shirt tucked into the beltless waistband of shiny grey pants with unhemmed bottoms that fell a few inches short of a new pair of white alligator golf shoes.

To Stony, he looked more like a pimp than a murderer; or perhaps he was just a bad dresser. He walked over to the bar, while his friends cowered slump-shouldered near the door.

"Two treesomes, Mr. Myron," he said, laying down some cash on the bar. Myron took the money, shaking his head as he turned to the cash register, mumbling to himself. He deposited the green fees and came back with a handful of scorecards.

"Remember, Slobeedobee," he said, "Everybody uses their own clubs." Then he tapped the side of the man's head. *"Comprendé?"*

When Myron touched the man, an expression flashed over his face that made Stony catch his breath. It was an expression that said, "I could kill you right now, then burn down your house."

But the glare lasted only a second before his amiable smile returned. "Okey-dokey," he said, joining his friends, who were still standing expressionless by the door. They walked quietly out, occasionally glancing behind them.

"Did you see the look that son of a bitch gave me," Myron said. "I noticed he didn't give you a badass look, Art."

Myron turned to Stony. "Last week that prick scraped your father's car with his pull cart and tried to walk away, thinking no one saw him." Myron started to laugh. "Next thing I know I see your old man chasing after this piece-of-shit yellow Ford Escort, catching up to old Slobeedobee and pulling him out of the car."

Stony's father laughed loudly. "What could I do?"

Stony and his father spent the next fifteen minutes finishing their Cokes and listening to Myron's theories on everything from aliens to midgets, the latter group for whom he had great sympathy. "Poor little bastards," he said.

By the time they got to the first tee, the first threesome of Serbs was on the green while the second was waiting in the fairway to hit their approach shots. "Let the morons finish up before we tee off," his father said. "That way we won't have to slow down." Stony agreed and they sat down on a yellow metal bench.

"You want to play for cash, Stony?" his father asked. "Is that what the big shots at the club do?"

Stony had been hoping the conversation wouldn't turn this way—comments about the "club," about the rich girls Stony was no doubt banging (though he was still a virgin), and about a wager. On the golf course, his father not only was hopelessly inferior to him but also a notoriously bad loser. Stony had witnessed a number of his terrible golf outings; the worse his father played the angrier and less focused he became. He once threw a whole set of golf clubs into the pond at the fourth hole, then tossed his golf shoes in after them.

"Let's just play for fun," Stony said.

"There's no such thing," his father replied. "Especially since I've gotten better."

"I just don't want to bet."

"That's what happens when a boy is raised by his mother," his father said, half-jokingly.

Stony felt his back go up. "Was there any other choice?"

"You can live with me any time you want, Stony," he said, which they both knew was a lie. "You're just dodging the bet," he added. "How about a dollar a hole. Just for fun."

"I said I don't want to."

His father walked over to his bag, withdrawing his driver like a sword, holding onto its club face, and jabbing the grip into Stony's side. "*En garde,*" he teased, challenging Stony. Then he began to cluck and flap his arms like a chicken.

Growing up, Stony had seen how his father could turn his substantial wit to evil purposes, and, as he continued to cluck, Stony felt an old anger rising up in him. He pushed away the grip of the driver and smiled. "Let's make it two dollars a hole," he said. "Just for the fun of it."

"That's my boy," his father crooned.

After Stony made the bet, he felt like crying. What was he thinking? He knew he'd win; he also knew his father was an even worse golfer under pressure. If there was more than one guy watching him tee off, he'd be sure to dub his drive.

"You go first," his father said.

The first hole was a short par four with a narrow fairway, guarded on the left by the road and on the right by a number of huge oak trees. Stony teed up and looked down the fairway, noticing the last threesome of Serbs walking off the green.

"Don't drive into those trees now, Stony," his father laughed.

Stony addressed his ball, swung and hit a high draw that carried the trees and landed in the middle of the fairway about sixty yards from the green.

"Big deal," his father said. "You have a lousy short game, anyway."

Stony didn't say a word, didn't even smile. He just stood next to the tee as his father readied himself. The only chance his father had to beat him was to play his own game, which was to hit two fairly short straight shots, chip to the green and try to one-putt for a par. But Stony's drive had obviously intimidated him. Instead of just punching out a short drive, he took a vicious swing, almost falling down, and they both watched as his ball sliced madly toward the trees. Stony almost laughed but then felt bad. "There's a lot of room there, dad," he said. "You'll probably have a shot to the green."

His father calmly returned his driver to the bag. "Listen," he said, "I don't need your cheerleading. We ain't at the club, okay?"

"Yeah, sure," Stony said, thinking, *And now it begins.* He walked down the fairway with his father, trying to make some small talk, but his father was fixed on the trees. When they got there, they found his ball. It was a good lie, but to reach the green, he would have to thread the shot through a five-foot opening between two thick tree trunks.

"I'd probably drop from there," Stony said. "I won't count the stroke and you can give me one later."

"Spare me," his father said, taking out a five iron from his bag. Stony sought protection behind a tree as his father addressed the ball and let it rip. The ball hit one tree on the left, careening into the trunk of another one on the right, and much to Stony's astonishment, it shot out onto the fairway. From there his father hit an eight iron a few feet to the left of the green. Then they both walked over to Stony's ball.

For his second shot, Stony hit a soft wedge about five feet from the pin. "You still have to make the putt," his father said, which he did after his father had chipped onto the green and one-putted for a five. "The important thing," his father said, "is that I didn't quit. I made you play your best. It's not just about money."

To reach the second hole they had to cross the road. In a sense, it was one of the easiest holes on the course, a three-hundred-and-twenty-five-yard par four with a lot of fairway to work with. But teeing off could be problematic. First, the driving tee was only about ten feet from the road. You could be in the middle of your downswing when a carload of punks might pass by and yell out, "Fore," "Fuck you, asshole," or "Faggot." One time someone even threw a beer bottle at Stony.

Secondly, about twenty yards from the tee was a four-foot wide trench with a big rock in the center of it. Any golfer could tap the ball over it, but to some, like his father, the trench acted like a magnet. Over the years, he had seen his father bang many balls into it, and rather than look for them, he'd just whack one after the other into its thin opening. So after Stony hit a long straight drive down the fairway, he could feel his shoulders tighten and breath quicken as his father prepared to tee off.

"Why don't you use an iron?" he suggested, thinking his father would hit the ball higher. "It's such a short hole, you don't really need the driver."

"The point," his father said, "if you remember anything I ever taught you, is to learn to use all your clubs." Then he took a vicious backswing and came down hard on the ball. It shot up swiftly, then dove toward the ditch. For a moment, all looked lost, until the ball crashed hard into the rock and shot about a hundred and fifty yards down the middle of the fairway. Stony exhaled and his father let out a loud "Yes." That shot lifted his father's spirits, and they both finished the hole with pars. As they were walking to the third hole, they passed all six Serbs who were tracking their balls on the fairway. Stony's father was visibly angry.

"What are you doing?" he said to one small man who

was in the process of picking up his ball from under a tree and throwing it into the fairway. The man just looked at him and shrugged. As he did, Stony's father confronted the one they called Slobeedobee.

"What the hell are you guys doing?" he asked. "You can't play with six guys."

"It's not six guys, Mr. Art," he said. "It's two treesomes." Then he walked quickly away, grinning, his new shoes sparkling under the bright sun.

"Well, we're driving into you, you bastard," his father yelled, hurrying to the next tee.

When they arrived there, Stony noticed that the Serbs, perhaps fearing his father, had picked up their balls and thrown them close to the green. "Relax, dad," he said, "they're way ahead. Even I couldn't reach them."

His father glared at Stony. "Even *you* couldn't reach them? What the fuck is that supposed to mean?" He ripped his driver out of his bag and grabbed a tee from his pocket. The ground was packed solid, so when he pushed the tee into the dirt, it broke. This happened three more times before one finally stayed planted. "Son of a bitch," he said, angry that he might not have a chance to drive into the Serbs.

The fairway of the third hole, flanked on both sides by a hundred yards of big oaks, was treacherous, but his father, with the Serbian targets clearly in his sights, hit one of the straightest and farthest drives of his career. The ball nearly reached the men, one of whom turned around and waved back, making his father even angrier. And this was how the third hole was played—in a rush, but with a cool single-mindedness that raised the level of play, for in their attempt to catch up to the Serbs, he and his father both parred the hole. His father's only disappointment came when they reached the fourth tee and discovered the

Serbs had already teed off.

Of all the holes at South Park, the fourth was the most intimidating. Between the tee and the green was a hundred and fifty yards of water, and if you carried it, you still had to deal with a twenty-yard-wide sand trap in front of the green and an asphalt road behind it. Over the years, Stony had seen the pond swallow many a ball, while others that were driven over the green bounced high off the road out of play. Many a golfer had thrown a club into the pond; many a golfer, incensed by his inability to carry the water, had driven ball after ball into its expanse until he had to be wrestled to the ground or led away trembling. Stony had rarely seen his father make it over the pond on the first try. But he knew today would be different, for when they reached the tee, the six Serbs were chipping onto the green from various places.

Stony's father went to his bag and emptied out all of his balls. Disappointed that he only had five, he asked Stony for more, and Stony unzipped the top pocket of his bag. His father reached into the slot, gathering about ten shiny new balls. "Bastards," he said, teeing up one after another and driving them into the air with his eight iron. His first shot arced high over the pond and landed in the middle of the green. When it hit, Stony could see all six Serbs flinch. His father's next shot faded in from the left, making one of the men cover up into the fetal position near the sand trap.

"Yes," he yelled. Even when he hit a low liner, it skipped the last twenty yards of the pond and nearly crippled another Serb. Ball after ball rained down upon them. With each shot, they scattered in different directions, until Slobeedobee decided to grab a ball and throw it into the pond, shaking his fist and yelling something unintelligible. The other men followed his lead, and so it went for a good five minutes: Stony's father hitting the balls, the men tossing them into the water. When all the balls were gone, his father smiled at Stony and said, "Did you see what those guys did, Stony? They threw our balls into the water. I think we should do something about that."

With a sick feeling in his stomach, Stony nodded, following his father through a wooded path that circled the pond. "Now don't pussy-out on me," his father said.

Chasing after him, Stony asked, "What are we going to do, beat up six guys?"

"Only if we have to," his father replied, picking up his pace. "I think if I take out Slobidowitz, the rest will scatter."

Take out? Stony thought.

"You're not thinking of pussying-out, are you?" his father repeated.

Pussying-out, Stony thought, shaking his head while trying to keep pace with his father. By the time they got to the green, all six Serbs had claimed it, standing around the pin, brandishing their putters. Stony's father reached for his driver, telling Stony to do the same. "This is ridiculous," Stony said.

"Just don't quit on me," his father yelled.

Before Stony could grab his driver, his father had jumped onto the green, scattering the Serbs. When they surrounded him, he waved the driver in circles, keeping them at bay. "Go get help," his father yelled, continuing to wave his club. "Go get Myron."

Stony could see the clubhouse a half a mile down the road. He ran toward it, trying to think as he ran. What could Myron do, he thought, or any of those old guys in the clubhouse? But then he saw the Grand Marquis in the parking lot, remembering that his father kept an extra key under the mat.

When he reached the car, he found the key and started the engine. Hendrix's primal yawp blasted out from the tape. The song was "Voodoo Child," and as Stony listened to the familiar lyrics, he shifted the car into reverse, then into drive, peeling out of the parking lot toward the fourth green. He gunned the engine once, twice, and as he approached the green, he saw his father, still swinging his driver in wide circles, glad that the cavalry had finally arrived.

Stony knew what the program called for: he was to drive the car onto the green and scare the hell out of the Serbs. It would be another mission, another story to add to the legend. But as he watched his father holding off the angry sixsome, a terrible thought flashed through his mind, and he knew that no matter how hard he might try, he wouldn't be able to turn the wheel. In an attempt to suppress the thought, he reached under the steering column and clicked on the amplifier switch, feeling the whole car tremble with Hendrix's guitar. He gunned the engine again and sped past the green, seeing his father's startled expression as the angry Serbs pounced upon him like a pack of starving hyenas.

I'M A MAN

▶ ▶ ▶ ▶ ▶

I WAS ON A RUN at the pool hall when my wife Nadia called and said to get to Zack's fast because Michele was a wreck. Michele wouldn't tell Nadia the problem, though we both knew it was Zack. But what now? Zack and I had been laid off for three months, and lately he'd been acting strange. In a way, I was sympathetic, though unemployment bothered him more than me. That's not to say I don't like working, but I see this layoff as a chance to take a well-earned rest and scout around. I've taken business courses at night and figure it might be time to look for a suit-and-tie job. I also heard Penney's might be training new store managers, and there's always insurance. I know I could make it big there.

But even though I have hope for the future—we all know the plant isn't going to call us back—waiting around for something to develop sometimes gets to me, like it was getting to Zack. Plus it's easy to feel guilty, knowing we're getting paid to play pool all afternoon and watch ESPN. Signing for the check even gets tough. I often wonder how my father and grandfather would've reacted to one of their own collecting unemployment. My father worked two jobs while I was growing up. He was a mailman by day and handled the crane at night. Sixteen hours a day for ten of his fifty-eight years. And my grandfather worked his entire adult life in the plant's manufacturing division where steel bars were cut and bent. Over a period of thirty years he inched his way up to be a supervisor. He was a notorious strikebreaker, not because he sided with management, but because he couldn't see alternatives to not working. Strikes were as unnatural and hateful to him as Liberace.

Zack's father and grandfather were also steelworkers, but he seemed more hung up on this than me, maybe because his father had been killed on the job. Squashed by a crane. Zack himself had an attitude similar to my grandfather's, which is why he dreads the days we sign for our checks. Michele told me he actually puked a few mornings waiting for me to pick him up. And at the unemployment office I can see him tense up as he stands in line, his back stiffening and rising like a cat's, sweat marks forming between his shoulder blades and under his armpits. After he signs, he walks straight out the door, pale-faced, unable to look at anyone. You'd think he was sneaking out of a whorehouse. And he gets mad when I want to hit Hogan's on the way home, thinking I'm lazy because I sleep until nine every morning and watch Oprah, or because I hang out at the pool hall. Once he told me that a man who doesn't work, who doesn't create something every day of his life is as "worthless as a used rubber."

In a way, I think he felt his new project was creative. He wanted to join a rock group. At the age of thirty-seven, laid off, unable to find a job, he decided to get young again through rock-and-roll. Some kids he coached in summer baseball were putting together a group and needed a singer. Zack became interested. He let his hair grow out and started to lift weights. He even found an old pair of leather pants in the attic he hadn't worn since his early twenties. They were a size too small, but he squeezed into them anyway. One night he wore these pants to the house for dinner, and I had to work hard not to laugh out loud.

At first I thought Zack was kidding about joining the group, but when I called Michele from the pool hall she said he was going over to William Kenski's garage that afternoon for band practice. Right then he was out shopping for a new harmonica and metal studs for his leather pants. In fairness to Zack, I thought he just wanted to help these kids or manage their group. Every summer he coached baseball for the 12-14-year-old league. And he was a good coach. My oldest son played on the team a few years ago, and later this summer my youngest will be catching for him. Zack's like an uncle to them, which is partly why I sympathize with him. But I also feel bad because lately Zack and Michele were having problems. They couldn't seem to make a baby, and this bothered Zack to no end. Since he'd been laid off, he'd spoken about it often. Zack and Michele were one of those couples who put off a family for ten years and when they finally wanted kids, they couldn't get the right juices flowing. It had to be tough on Zack. To use his words, I know I would've felt as "worthless as a used rubber" if Nadia and I couldn't have had kids. And it was Zack's fault. I got the impression he was shooting blanks, though Michele only tells me so much.

I left the pool hall right after I called Michele. The air outside was hot and wet compared to the dry, air-conditioned pool hall. I wasn't looking forward to the drive—the hot vinyl car seats, the inescapable smell and taste of exhaust and ore dust. When I got to Zack's, Michele answered the door in a white, knee-length, terrycloth bathrobe. Her straight blond hair was damp and combed back over her shoulders. She put her arms around me, pressing her chin into my chest. "What are we going to do, Jake?" she asked. "What are we going to do?" I closed the door behind me and comforted her.

About half an hour later we were having coffee in the kitchen. Michele sat across from me, turning her coffee mug around in circles with her slender fingers. In spite of her obvious sadness, she looked pretty. She was three years younger than Zack, though she could've passed for twenty-five. She wore her white nurse's uniform now, making her look even younger. Like Nadia, she seemed to maintain the curves and ruddy complexion of youth, while Zack and I had thickened from head to toe.

She looked up from her mug, her green eyes saddening. "I feel it's my fault," she said.

"It's nobody's fault. Just let him get it out of his system. He's lost, like a lot of guys right now." That sounded like good advice.

"But what if he's serious? My God, could you see him singing at junior high school dances or parties? He looked pathetic when he left here in those leather pants. He's scaring me. Maybe he knows things."

I must admit I didn't view the situation that seriously. I even thought it was a bit funny. I was sure Zack would go to a few band practices, have some fun, and blow off steam, but he was too smart to take this thing seriously. He was using the rock group to feel young again, the way a man might use a woman.

"It's okay," I told her. "You'll see." Then I said things would change soon and that I had heard rumors at the pool hall about the plant recalling guys. That, unfortunately, was a lie. "We'll just all hang in there," I said.

She seemed annoyed. "Why do you go to that creepy place?"

"Better than singing with a rock group of fourteen year

olds, I guess."

"Don't enjoy this too much, Jake."

"I'm not."

"You're the only one I can count on. He'll listen to you."

"I know," but I really didn't. Although I was the closest thing Zack had to a best friend, I knew he didn't respect certain things about me.

"So go and talk to him. It's only one-thirty. Band practice doesn't start until two o'clock." She stood up and carried her coffee mug over to the sink. Her back was to me as she rinsed the mug under the faucet. She had the long, firm back and strong shoulders of a swimmer. I came up behind her and placed my mug on the sink, then pressed my chest softly against her, feeling her buttocks touching my thighs. I put my arms around her waist, moving my hands up toward her breasts. Her clean hair smelled like things green and growing.

She turned the water off, leaving the mug in the sink, then tilted back her head and said, "Not now, Jake. Please go talk to him. I feel horrible as it is." She wasn't fighting me but I knew she was right.

William Kenski was the leader of the rock group. I knew very little about him except that he was the first baseman on Zack's team last year and a very mediocre hitter. He wasn't the kid you wanted at the plate with two outs in the ninth and the winning run on third. I did know William's mother, though, and I didn't like her. She was a tall, fat Slavic woman who yelled at umpires when they called strikes on her son. She brought a hibachi to every game, cooking hot dogs for her and her husband on a grassy area in front of the small green bleachers. During a game, she'd be eating a hot dog with one hand, and with the other she'd be shaking an enormous fork at the umpire. The jam session was in the Kenski's garage, so I wasn't very happy when I pulled into the driveway and saw Ruth Kenski raking freshly cut grass on the front lawn. I got out of the car. She was smiling.

"You looking for Zack?" she asked.

"Yep."

"He's in the garage waiting for the other boys." She emphasized the word "boys," but I ignored her, moving toward the garage.

"Hey, wait," she said. "I wanna ask you somethin'." I turned and saw her leaning on the rake, her fleshy thighs oozing out of a pair of dirty white shorts. With her free hand she was pointing to the side of her head, spinning one fat finger in circles. "Is he nuts or something? He ain't going to hurt nobody, is he?"

"Of course not."

She shook her head. "What's happening to some people? Him. You, too," she yelled, surprising me a bit. "You think we're all deaf and dumb?"

"You finished?"

"Just get that crazy fool out of here. Leather pants. Jesus." She made the sign of the cross as I walked away.

The large, pull-down garage door was locked, so I went through the side door, grateful to be out of the sun. Zack was standing alone at a microphone, fooling around with his harmonica, which, to be honest, he could play fairly well. He was surrounded on both sides by guitars and amplifiers, and behind him was a cheap-looking set of drums. One look at him and it was easy to see why Michele had called. He wore his leather pants and a skin-tight white T-shirt with a pack of cigarettes jammed into the pocket over his left breast. He had greased and combed his hair straight back, and he'd bought a pair of black wrap-around sunglasses. He was enjoying himself, stomping one foot, playing a few old blues progressions. He saw me and stopped. He was smiling.

"Paid for your ticket of admission, Jake?" He held out his arms and spun around. "What do you think? A Paul Butterfield look-a-like?"

"This is a joke, right?"

He blew a few notes on the harmonica, not looking up at me. "If you say so."

"Would you take the glasses off a minute?" I asked. When he did, I expected to see deep black circles around his eyes, half-believing a number of sleepless nights had brought him to this silly end. But he looked well rested, alert.

"What's up?"

"Michele asked me to talk to you."

"That's curious. What about?"

"What do you think?"

He kept smiling. "Hey, she's getting upset over nothing." He motioned me over to a card table set up next to the bass guitar. We sat down. "Look," he said. "I'm just having some fun."

"That's what I told her."

"But consider this, Jake. Who's to say I couldn't sing for a real group. Look how old Jagger is."

"You're kidding?"

"What're you so worried about?"

"I'm worried about my son going to a junior high dance and seeing Uncle Zack jiggling his middle-aged body around the stage, or about people thinking you're weird, you know, the coach who likes little boys. And we're all worried about Michele."

"Ah, you're a very special person, Jake. I appreciate it."

"I didn't have to come here, you know."

He was still smiling, very calm and relaxed. "Yeah, I

understand, what with all the interesting things going down at the pool hall on a Wednesday afternoon." His smile broadened. "Relax, I'm not going to sing at dances or take little boys into the woods. But what's the harm? I'm just honing my talents. The kids know that. They know I'm just having fun."

"But why the outfit?"

He didn't answer, and it was obvious that he was done talking. In a way, I didn't mind because I wanted to get out of the garage before the rest of the band came. I had accomplished my purpose. I could tell Michele that, yes, Zack was reliving his adolescence, but he wasn't crazy.

When Zack stood in front of the microphone again, sunglasses back on, I got up to leave. "Wait a second," he said. "Catch this action." He began to play a blues progression that sounded familiar to me. "*I'm a Man,*" he said. "Remember? Bo Diddley. Listen and tell me what you think." He crouched over the dead microphone and in between bursts of the harmonica he sang the lyrics to the song, blowing wildly into the instrument, keeping his right leg stationary while his left leg gyrated like Elvis'. His leather pants stretched, threatening to explode like a water balloon, and his tight T-shirt couldn't keep the inch or two of flab on his waist from quivering. I started toward the door, then turned to take a last look. He waved to me, still blowing away. "I'm a man," he sang, "I spell M...," but I was out the door before he could finish.

When I left Zack I was depressed. I drove by the plant, listening to the familiar rumble of railroad cars, the banging of steel on steel. I thought about Zack, Nadia, Michele, and me. I wanted to talk to Michele or to Nadia, but they were at work, so I drove in the direction of the pool hall. When I got there I bought a Coke and felt better. The place had gotten crowded with other guys from the plant and high school sharpshooters who couldn't find summer jobs.

I looked for and found my favorite pool cue. I chalked its tip, twirling the wooden shaft in my palm, deciding it was senseless to worry about Zack and ruin my day. I scanned the rows of green-topped billiard tables, listening to the hard music of ball hitting ball. A familiar competitive urge filled my insides, and I felt confident I'd win back the five dollars I'd lost that morning.

THE MORE THINGS CHANGE

TWO POLICE CARS were parked piggyback, their flashing red lights slicing through the silhouettes of neighbors who'd gathered outside Fred's house. Everyone, except the police, looked half-asleep, though there was a white-haired woman in her bathrobe quizzing two of the officers. She tried to restrain her two Yorkshire terriers with one hand while holding an umbrella over her head with the other. Annoyed by the lights and the people, the dogs tried to break from their leashes, yelping into the thick, evening mist. One policeman scrutinized me as I approached. He was overweight and smelled like a cigar, the kind of cop who stops you for a spot-check, hoping to catch a glimpse of thigh, or just needing to wave his gun in some woman's face.

"You going to leave your car there?" he asked.

As I came closer and told him who I was, one of the terriers leapt at me, and the old woman jerked its leash. "They won't hurt you, honey," she said. "They're good babies."

"He wants to see you," the officer explained, loudly enough to make everyone look at me, especially the old woman, who was trying to piece things together.

"You're awfully young," she said.

I looked at the house, a small ranch separated from the

road by what used to be a lawn. The one time I was here, Fred had explained how he was dying every day and didn't want to waste time cutting the grass, so he dug it up, covered the dirt with wood chips, and placed a large white, concrete birdbath in the center. Beyond the birdbath, through the thin drapes of a living-room window, I could see the shadow of a figure appearing and disappearing, as if offering his head for target practice.

"He's going to blow his head off," the cop said. "He wanted you here."

"I hardly know him. Strange."

"Don't tell me about strange. Last week we busted a fisherman who cut off his wife's ring finger with a steak knife because she was fooling around. He ground it up in the garbage disposal and was sitting in a corner laughing when we got there." He waited for my reaction, apparently ready to convince me with more stories if necessary.

"What I'm saying is that I just worked with him."

"That might be, but you certainly knew how to get here."

The outline of the head reappeared in the window. "I was here for an office party once. I haven't worked with him for six months."

The old woman moved closer and told the officer she hadn't seen me around. "It's probably money problems," she said. "The poor man's probably broke. Look at the lawn." She emphasized the last word, which sent her dogs into a yelping match.

The cop placed his hand on his gun. "The point," he said, "is that the man says he has a gun, and he's going to smoke himself." He looked at me. "He wants you here. So what happens next?"

I glanced again at the shadow in the window, and the cop removed his cap, obviously annoyed. He was getting wet and probably wished he was home watching HBO movies. He said I could wait in the squad car, then hesitated. "One other thing," he said. "Do you know Trevor Anderson? He wanted us to call him, too."

I was six months out of my marriage when I began working for Fred. He had been at the body shop for about a year, brought in by the Old Man to expand business, or at least get it back to where it was. When the Old Man turned seventy, he had decided to sit back and let his two sons take over, which turned out to be a mistake.

Fred had explained the situation differently when he interviewed me. He said the shop was going through a "revitalization" period, and I remember thinking how mechanical the language of business was. I had been a teacher for six years before I moved to Buffalo, so Fred couldn't understand why I wanted to work at a body shop.

When a man and woman meet for the first time, there is always a sizing-up period, whether it be for seconds or minutes, a moment when one hovers between extremes of attraction and repulsion. When I met Fred, I felt as if I had tumbled into an abyss. His every movement, every gesture, seemed forced, mechanical. He was dressed rather shabbily in an old grey suit, and his pant cuffs were hiked up a few inches above his ankles, so that his poverty of appearance mirrored his poverty of spirit.

I did various chores for Fred from answering phones to working the cash register. From what I could gather, Fred managed to retrieve much of the clientele the Old Man's sons had lost, and his advertisements in the *Buffalo News* were bringing in new business. In terms of body shops, this one was better than average; the Old Man's sons couldn't add two and two and had all the social graces of bears in heat, but they were good at unbending bumpers and planing fiberglass.

From talking to customers, I also learned that Trevor did his share to keep them coming back. He was an artist. The men with expensive cars—those pointed, penile sports cars with the condom-like leather covers over the headlights—had an exaggerated admiration for Trevor, the kind of childlike admiration men give to famous athletes. My ex-husband once said that he'd gladly exchange his small retail business for the ability to dunk a basketball like Michael Jordan. This kind of man would leave his car for a week or more and rent another one to accommodate Trevor's schedule. They'd wait for him the way some women wait for their favorite hairdresser. Once, a short salesman with fat lips, a perm, and a body overdeveloped by Nautilus tipped Trevor fifty dollars for getting his white BMW ready before his company's next convention in Toronto. He said he had a "Chink" girlfriend there he wanted to impress. Trevor took the money, winked at me, and said, "One more soul gone to hell for sins of the flesh."

The man thoughtfully eyed Trevor, obviously trained by his company to nurture any potential customer's crazy idea. "Yeah," he answered. "I never thought of it that way."

When he left, Trevor leaned over the counter and whispered, "He'll be the first to go when the revolution comes." I laughed, and when I turned around, I could see Fred staring at us through the long, rectangular glass window separating his office from mine.

Fred would grant that customers liked Trevor's work, but he thought Trevor moved too slowly. The only time I went to lunch with Fred, I told him that Trevor's slowness was offset by the business he brought in, but Fred wouldn't hear it. "You protect him like he's your father," he said, surprised at his own boldness. That was the first time Fred gave me the creeps; the second time was on my birthday.

I came to know Trevor fairly well through lunches. The body shop was only a few blocks from the lake, and at noon, while Tony, the Old Man's youngest son, and the other men went for a beer at a local tavern, Trevor and I would bring our lunches to the waterfront. It was spring, the early afternoons heating up, and we'd eat our sandwiches while sitting on the rocks that separated the lake from a parking lot and marina.

Fred was right when he said Trevor was old enough to be my father. He was fifty-seven, well over six feet tall, broad-shouldered, with the barreled chest of a wrestler. He always wore blue, cotton work shirts over a white T-shirt, a fringe of grey hair puffing out around his collar. His face was broad, his forehead cresting over his eyes like a slab of granite. In a way, he reminded me of every working-class father or grandfather I had grown up around, except that he had been formally educated, and his intelligence came across in his eyes and hands. When he spoke, his eyes would drift to the left, as if searching for a word or idea. And his hands didn't seem to fit his muscular, hairy arms. They were small, his fingers slender; perhaps intelligent is the best word to describe them.

Trevor told me he had grown up in South Buffalo; he had left; he had studied sculpture and worked in that medium, teaching at a small college in Kentucky for ten years; he had come home because something started to "hurt awful bad inside." He had thought he was dying because his dreams kept telling him so, but it was his wife who died—of cancer—though he wouldn't say much about her. He lived alone in a small house he rented in Hoover Beach; he never invited me there, but I went once on my own.

It was sometime before I could convince the policeman to let me approach the house and speak with Fred. He said he preferred to wait until the "shrink" arrived, but I assured him that Fred wasn't the kind of man to own a gun. There were police procedures, of course, but he eventually went with his instincts, holding an umbrella over us as we crossed the street. When we reached the sidewalk, Fred's shadow appeared behind the drapes. We came closer, walking on the wet wood chips. When we reached the birdbath, Fred spoke through a screen window, and the officer let go of my arm. I heard some murmuring from the neighbors behind me.

"Marilyn?" Fred asked, almost in a whisper.

"Yes," I replied.

He moved the drapes to the side, and I could spy the pointed chin, high cheekbones, bulging eyes, and the high forehead always in the state of chronic contraction when he spoke. Every show of emotion—words, movements—had always seemed painful for Fred. His body language would be best described as choppy, the syntax of his movements as disjointed as a wooden puppet's.

"I want to apologize," he said, and I thought he was talking about Trevor's firing. "I want to apologize for your accident. For your foot."

At first, I didn't understand what he meant, but then it came to me—my date with a podiatrist named Steven, the rocks, my broken foot. I wanted to grab the officer's gun and fire wildly toward the window. But I didn't have the chance. I don't know if Fred sensed my feelings, as crazy people do, or if my face, illuminated by the porch light, showed its anger. But he suddenly placed his entire frame in the window. His head rested on his left shoulder, as if he'd been hung, and his arms lay limply at his sides. At the end of his right arm, a revolver dangled. The officer and I jumped back, and Fred disappeared. Back at the car, I noticed the rain was coming down harder, and I remembered Trevor telling me one stormy day that I could avoid the drops if I walked sideways.

After my divorce, I didn't confide in many people. My friends and family still think I'm in denial and will eventually come unglued, but I don't agree. I'm just on the move, trying things out, avoiding the drops as much as possible, and to do this, I had to leave the proof of my failure, which clung to every couch, chair, and bedspread in my house. I had explained this feeling to Trevor, but he thought I would stop "running."

"There are enough good men around," he said, "even here." And he asked if I were seeing anyone.

In a way, I was seeing a podiatrist named Steven, who somehow had broken away from his Jewish mother in New York and was caring for the feet of suburban lawyers and bankers who daily jogged themselves into oblivion. Steven was a nice diversion, and he made me a good pair of orthotics. He also enrolled us in a ballroom dancing class at Buffalo State, and afterwards he'd treat me to a brownie and espresso at Starbucks.

I had been working at the shop for a month when the flowers came. It was my birthday, but I made a point not to tell anyone. I hate birthdays. At first I thought the flowers were from Steven, which bothered me, because I had made the nature of our relationship clear. There was a one-word note, "Heartfelt," and I racked my brain to discover a secret meaning behind it. Had I ever heard it before? All the men in the shop looked at me through the glass partition, and I could hear a few good-natured laughs. Tony was applauding, the same Tony who earlier in the day had told me that the best time to "hit on" a woman was after she got her hair cut because she felt insecure. There wasn't much for me to do but to place the flowers on my desk and go about my business.

At break time, Trevor denied sending them. Later I called Steven, who swore he didn't send them. Finally, I phoned the florist, who said he'd been asked to keep the name a secret. I even called my mother to find out if she had told my ex-husband where I was working, but she hadn't. He wasn't the flower-giving type, anyway, and the last I had heard he was on his second nymphet, a twenty-year-old grocery clerk.

I also remember the day I received the flowers because it was the same day Trevor nearly got fired. It was a warm May afternoon, a preview of summer, when the humidity is low and there are enough clouds rolling in to make the sun bearable. Trevor and I went to the lakefront and talked. I asked him how long he would continue to work at the Old Man's, and he said until he died. I thought that was sad.

"This is home," he said.

"To me, it's a kind of death," I said, hoping I didn't offend him.

"Why?"

"The same thing every day."

"But it's not. He peeled back the bread on his baloney sandwich, exposing the mustard layered on it. "Yesterday I had mayonnaise and baloney. How much change do you want?"

"But where are those guys in the shop going?" I added.

"And if you put Fred into the real world, he'd get devoured."

"You're wrong. He'd be an advisor to the President."

I laughed. "He's really tragic," I said.

"But he likes you."

"What?"

"He watches you."

We returned to the shop a little late. All the workers were back, and Fred was keeping watch from behind his desk. I often thought that when everyone else went to lunch, Fred leaned back in his chair, flicking out his tongue at passing flies and insects. Trevor and I received a few catcalls from the men, especially Tony. Then, for some reason, just before Trevor and I went our separate ways, I told him it was my birthday. I was surprised when he gave me a big hug. The whole shop erupted good-naturedly, and Tony yelled that it was obvious who had sent the flowers. The whole scene would have been funny, except that Fred stormed out of his office.

"Lunch is over," was all he said, and this comment seemed to annoy Trevor. Lately, Fred had been criticizing him, saying he wasn't carrying his weight.

"What?" he asked.

"Lunch is over," Fred repeated.

"An aphorism from one of the great wits of our time," Trevor said.

"It was my fault," I said to Fred, standing between him and Trevor.

"I didn't ask you," he said, trembling.

Trevor took a step toward him, and that was the first time I ever saw him angry. It was also the first time I ever heard him swear. "Back off, Fred," he said, "or I'll tear off your head and stick it up your ass." Tony found this comment extraordinarily funny, which angered Fred even more.

"If you don't like it, talk to my superiors," Fred said.

Trevor took another step, and I tried to restrain him. "That's 99% of Buffalo," he said.

Everyone laughed, and Fred raised his fist at Trevor like a little child. To everyone's surprise, including my own, he took a swing into the air, knocking the flowers off my desk. Trevor went after him, but Tony and some of the other men restrained him before he could damage Fred, who ran out of the building. Water and flowers were all over the floor, and as I cleaned up the mess, I realized Trevor's days were numbered. I also realized who had sent the flowers.

The two weeks after my birthday weren't very pleasant for Trevor or Fred. After his confrontation with Trevor, Fred phoned the Old Man, who actually made an appearance. When I heard people speak of the Old Man, I pictured an enormous Paul Bunyan-like figure straightening out bumpers with his bare teeth. Instead, this little Italian man showed up. If he had any teeth, you couldn't see them; he was thin but muscular and he wore wire-rimmed glasses. He looked like a hunchback when he walked and he rarely looked up, the only visible motion of his face being the chomping of his gums.

When he hobbled into the shop, Tony and his brother, Enzio, gave him a big welcome. The Old Man mumbled something in Italian, then waved them off as if they were bad schoolboys. Trevor was working on the door of a blue Volvo and never looked up. The Old Man went over to him, crouched down, and placed a hand on his shoulder. They talked and laughed, and it was obvious they went back a long way. Then the Old Man stood and shuffled into Fred's office, closing the door behind him. There was a short conversation and he left.

After seeing the Old Man, I felt Trevor had no worries; their obvious friendship and what appeared to be mutual respect would protect him. But the following days proved me wrong. Fred became belligerent, trying to provoke Trevor. It was as if whatever manhood he possessed had been offended, and since he couldn't take Trevor outside and box him, he tried intimidation. He would stand next to Trevor and criticize his work; sometimes he'd send him home early without pay. One day his criticisms became so severe that even Tony told him to lay off. Fred also developed a strange physical posture. Trevor had threatened him physically, so Fred's male chromosomes responded as best they could, contorting his skeletal frame when he was in Trevor's presence. He would lean over him, thrusting out his pointed chin, his hands clasped behind his back. He tried to push his chest out, but it was hopeless, and it would have been funny if the whole scenario didn't suggest an ominous fate for Trevor.

During this period, I was still seeing Steven. After ballroom dancing lessons, after Starbucks, he would take me home and ask to come in. I always politely refused; it was my way of keeping him at a distance. He didn't seem to mind, though he insisted on waiting in the car until I got safely inside. On one particular night, I noticed that the porch light was out. I walked very carefully, and about ten feet from the door, I stumbled over what appeared to be a few small stones, then turned my ankle on something very large. I heard a crack and went down. Steven helped me into the house, almost stumbling himself.

When he opened the door and turned on the light, all he could say was "Jesus." We both looked at the walkway, which was covered with stones—some small, some large. I was in too much pain at the time to realize that someone—most likely neighborhood kids, I thought—had played a practical joke.

After I had the cast put on, I was home a few days. On my first day back, I heard Trevor had been fired. This was how Tony told the story. The day after my accident, Fred explained what had happened, concealing the details, though he certainly knew them. When Trevor asked for particulars Fred told him to mind his own business. I could picture Fred, chin and chest out, assaulting Trevor with the only weapon he had: me. He was indeed acting like a jealous lover, and I will never forget how sickened I was by that knowledge, how concerned that, like my mother, I attracted a certain kind of man. My father didn't look like Fred, but he was a brooder, a walking time bomb, and when he came home, even inanimate objects seemed to swell with anxiety. Once, when I was six or seven, my mother and father and I went to visit my uncle in the hospital. We were standing in the elevator with another man, who started joking with my mother. When he got off on the next floor, my father accused her of flirting. "Just remember," he yelled, "I'm the one who takes you to bed."

Perhaps Trevor sensed a similar sickness in Fred and that's why he became infuriated when Fred refused to give the details of the accident. According to Tony, Trevor took out a sheet of paper, wrote something on it, and gave it to Fred. He said it was the name of a good psychiatrist. That's when Fred pushed Trevor, though I have trouble believing that. He probably became nervous, tripped over a sander, and fell into Trevor. As the story goes, Trevor hit him once in the face and was officially fired.

I tried to call Trevor at home, but no one answered. I asked Fred for his number, but he said to mind my own business. Tony overheard the conversation and walked into Fred's office, pushing him aside. He removed Trevor's folder from a filing cabinet and wrote down his address for me.

I was unfamiliar with Trevor's neighborhood, so I stopped at a gas station for directions, then drove to his home as I had been driving all day, careful not to let the cast on my left foot get jammed beneath the brake pedal. I arrived at a small, winterized cottage and felt relief when I saw Trevor's car in the driveway parked behind an old, yellow Volkswagen Rabbit.

With the help of my crutches, I made it to Trevor's door, astonished when a beautiful young redhead greeted me. She also seemed surprised, but recognized my name and let me in. Trevor was sitting on an old, wooden rocker, dressed in his work clothes. He jumped up and helped me to the rocker; then he placed his arm around the young woman. "This is Julie," he said, "my youngest daughter. She's visiting for a few weeks." She smiled at him, and I thought about my own father, sitting comatose in front of the TV, refusing to take Lithium because it constipated him, my mother his willing nurse. For a while no one knew what to say, then Trevor admitted he'd been fired.

"Call the Old Man," I said.

"I did. He can't do much."

"He owns the place," I said.

"He doesn't want to deal with it any more. That's why he turned it over to Fred. What can he do? Give it back to his kids to ruin? He's tired. I understand."

"You understand too much," his daughter said. "They're all a bunch of assholes."

Trevor put his hand on her shoulder. "I have enough friends," he said. I'll manage."

"How?" I asked.

"Rest awhile," he said. "Maybe visit an old friend in California and do some fishing. Why don't you stay for dinner?"

I did and had a surprisingly nice evening. At Trevor's request, we didn't mention his firing again; instead, we talked about my teaching background and his daughter's latest trip to Nova Scotia. She was getting her doctorate in oceanography. At the end of the evening, I said goodbye and didn't see Trevor for a few months, until after he returned from California. He took me to dinner one night, then disappeared. Even though I hardly saw him outside of work, I was devastated. In September, when a teaching position opened at a suburban high school, I quit the shop. I phoned Fred, wanting to call him every name I could think of, but I didn't have the energy. I had felt the same way when I left my husband.

After Fred's mock suicide, the cop and I walked back to the squad car, and I told him I'd had enough.

"You better stay, lady. You might be useful."

"Can you make me?" I asked.

He thought for a moment, rubbing his stomach with his free hand, the other hand clutching his umbrella. "No, I guess not. But won't you feel bad if he shoots himself?"

"No."

As the rain came down harder, bystanders headed for their homes. If Fred was going to kill himself, there wouldn't be much of an audience. But the lady with the Yorkshires hung on until the very end, and when I told the cop "No," she looked startled and said, "How sad." I had this rush of anger and an urge to kick one of her "babies," but instead I wished the cop good luck and walked away.

The sky began to thunder mightily as I headed toward my car. I collapsed into the driver's seat and pulled away, fighting off a perverse desire to glance back at Fred's house. I had no idea where I was going, and I thought about my father. After years of psychologically tormenting the family, he had a manic-depressive episode and never recovered. The last time I went home, I watched his routine. He'd get up in the morning, walk to the market, and buy a newspaper. Then he'd sit in the car all day and read.

I pressed down harder on the accelerator, trying to escape this memory, not slowing down until I came to a stop sign. I made a left off Fred's street, the sky exploding with light, nearly forcing me off the road. Then I saw a brighter flash, accompanied by a large boom, as if some giant, celestial cannon had gone off.

Peter Johnson was born in Buffalo, New York in 1951. He received his B.A. from the State University of New York at Buffalo and his M.A. and Ph.D. in English from the University of New Hampshire. His previous books include *Miracles & Mortifications*, which won the 2001 James Laughlin Award given by the Academy of American Poets; *Pretty Happy!*; and a chapbook of poems, *Love Poems for the Millennium*. In 1999 he received a fellowship from the National Endowment for the Arts and in 2002 received a fellowship from the Rhode Island Council for the Arts. He is also the founding editor of *The Prose Poem: An International Journal* and editor of *The Best of The Prose Poem: An International Journal*, published by White Pine Press in 2000. A contributing editor to *American Poetry Review*, *Web del Sol*, and *Slope*, Peter Johnson teaches at Providence College. He lives in Rhode Island with his wife, Genevieve, and sons Kurt and Lucas.